"Say my name again, *chérie,* as you would call to your lover."

"Please, Jacques!" Janine couldn't tell what she was pleading for in that moment. Her breath caught in her throat as his hands on her shoulders pulled her to him. His mouth touched hers in a gentle, tentative kiss that became more demanding as it deepened.

The long kiss left them both breathless. His lips traveled over her cheeks and she closed her eyes. When he kissed her eyelids, she could feel her eyes pulsating under his touch like captured butterflies.

"You have the darkest and longest eyelashes I've ever seen. In the sun, their curve casts a shadow on your cheekbones and frames your eyes like amethyst on velvet," Jacques murmured. "Oh, Janine, please let me love you now . . ."

Belgian Romance

Lucinda Anne Day

GOLDEN APPLE PUBLISHERS

BELGIAN ROMANCE

A Golden Apple Publication / June 1985

Golden Apple is a trademark of Golden Apple Publishers

All rights reserved.

Copyright © 1984 by Lucinda Anne Day.
Cover photograph by Photofile.
This book may not be reproduced in whole or in part, by
mimeograph or any other means, without permission.
For information address: Golden Apple Publishers,
666 Fifth Avenue, New York, New York 10103.

ISBN 0-553-19773-8

PRINTED IN THE UNITED STATES OF AMERICA

O   0 9 8 7 6 5 4 3 2 1

One

The late-morning sun beat down mercilessly on the Belgian country road and from time to time Janine Heerlen changed sides to take advantage of whatever shade was available in the July heat. After an enjoyable two weeks on the French Riviera, Orpe Le Petit, where she had arrived two days earlier to meet and become acquainted with her aunt and uncle, offered very few diversions. Exercising the dog was one of the few activities that met with Pierre and Laure Heerlen's approval. Janine had thought she would stay with her relatives for a week before visiting Paris prior to her return to Kansas City, but she knew she wouldn't last there more than another day or so. Even her planned trip to nearby Brussels had met with objections from Laure, who insisted that her niece couldn't miss the one-o'clock lunch around which the Heerlens' day revolved.

Her red sundress clinging to the overheated skin of her slim young body, Janine rubbed her hand between her high, firm breasts to soak up the perspiration as she watched Heidi fetch the ball she had thrown. They hadn't passed a house for half a mile, and Janine was getting ready to pitch the ball once more when the Doberman turned onto a path lined by poplars.

Grateful for the shade, Janine followed the dog and listened to the incessant buzzing of insects in the waist-high yellow weeds bordering the dusty lane. Realizing she was on the land that used to belong to her ancestors, the land that Uncle Pierre had pointed out to her the preceding day from the living-room window, Janine wondered if her father had walked this same lane with his dog when he was a child. Then Heidi ran back to her and she threw the ball again.

There was a splash, and, thinking the ball must have landed in a ditch, she hurried around the curve. The path ended at a secluded pond. By the near shore was a weeping willow. On the opposite bank, pink water lilies shimmered in the sun like a Monet canvas. Inhaling the scent of wild mint and honeysuckle, Janine listened to the song of a thrush cascading its trilling notes.

Heidi looked from Janine to the clear water of the pond. Shielding her eyes from the glare, she peered into the depths. The red ball was a miniature sun winking in the shadows cast by the willow. Slipping off her white sandals, she waded into the pond, but before she could reach the ball, the white sandy bottom dropped away sharply and she knew she would have to swim for it. Dismissing the thought that Laure and Pierre would certainly disapprove of their twenty-two-year-old niece swimming without a bathing suit, Janine threw her dress on the bank and jumped in. The cool water made her tingle with pleasure.

She dived under and picked up the ball, shaking her curly black hair when she surfaced. Treading water, she laughed at Heidi's eager stance in the shallows, and had just pitched the ball to her when she heard a rhythmic, reverberating sound. As she swam toward her clothes, she realized that the thumping noise came from a horse's hooves, and suddenly she knew she couldn't regain the shore in time to dress. Quickly she swam to the overhanging willow-tree branches, hoping the intruder would gallop on across the field. But she soon realized there was no chance she would go unnoticed, because Heidi, running back and forth on the shore, wouldn't stop barking.

Laughter echoed in her leafy shelter and a man said in

French, "It's all right, old girl. Nobody'll hurt you or your mistress."

Janine peered through the leaves. In a white polo shirt, blue riding britches, and soft black leather boots, the horseman looked like a marauding Viking. He bent over the neck of his magnificent chestnut stallion, lifted her red sundress from the grass with his riding crop, and waved it above his head like a banner. He laughed again, his white teeth flashing in his suntanned face, and cantered his horse in a circle at the foot of the path, his burnished blond hair shimmering in the sun.

Janine thought he was the most handsome man she had ever seen and wished she could have met him under more conventional circumstances. Then, at the sight of her dress waving in the air like a challenge, the reality of her predicament made her shout, "Put that down!" As soon as she spoke, she bit her lip. Her outburst had given away her cover.

"Ah, my mysterious naiad has an accent." He reined in his horse and looked toward Janine's hiding place.

"I'm doing my best to lose it, and you're not being very polite," she replied, clutching some branches about her chest. The leaves tickled her bare skin.

"Your accent is charming, but your defensiveness makes me glad you're not Artemis, or you would destroy me for coming upon you at your bath," he said, while Heidi barked and leaped about the stallion's hooves.

"Can't you see this is neither the time nor the place for a lecture in Greek mythology?" She smiled in spite of herself. She had meant to spend the summer practicing her French so she would be ready for her first teaching position in the fall, but this was a ridiculous way to improve her skills.

"Unfortunately, I see nothing. I can only imagine."

In frustration, she reverted to English and shouted, "Just split! Go! Get lost!"

"I knew that if I waited, more information would be forthcoming. With that stream of slang, you just told me you're an American." He examined the sundress. "And you wear a size seven and are very young." Burying his nose in the red folds, he added," And you favor a clean, elusive scent. Is it wisteria or lavender? I like it." He had spoken in English. Except for the way he pronounced his r's, his accent was flawless, and his voice, in its deeper registers, seemed to weave a spell in the sunny glade.

A shiver ran down Janine's spine. With his handsome face and athletic physique, the intimate gesture and the subtle throaty burr of his r's, he was incredibly seductive. Trying to keep her voice firm, she called, "You've had your fun and I suspect that's in short supply in Orpe Le Petit. Will you ride on now?" She really wanted to add, *But don't go too far. Just give me a chance to get dressed.* She could see he was still grinning, the smile lifting one corner of his mouth and accentuating the cleft in his chin. He reminded her of a faun. Or was it a centaur?

"I'm wondering if you know you're asking me to get off my own land, mystery girl."

At this statement, Janine realized that the stranger was Jacques Laurent. She searched her mind to remember what Laure had told her, but all she could recall now was that the Heerlens leased their café from him and that he was one of the wealthiest men in the country.

"Monsieur Laurent?" She addressed him tentatively.

"That's not fair. You know my name and won't tell me yours."

Janine watched him dismount, removing both black-booted feet from the stirrups simultaneously, throwing his right leg forward over the stallion's neck, and jumping to the ground in a fluid motion. Her admiration for his agility was short-lived, however. In fascinated horror she saw Heidi lunge for her sundress. As Jacques pulled one way and the Doberman another, the dress ripped apart. Janine covered her eyes and retreated among the reeds by the bank, wondering wildly if she could weave a grass skirt in which to walk home. Her feet sunk in squishy, oozing mud and she felt the rushes twine around her ankles like water snakes. She screamed and lost her balance.

His deep, musical voice was very close when he asked, "Are you all right?" The reeds hid him from view.

"I will be, as soon as I can free myself," she replied, uncoiling some roots from her thigh.

"I'm sorry about your clothes," he said. He sounded contrite.

She saw what remained of her sundress dangling from his hand not a foot away from her face and realized there wasn't enough left to cover her body with. She wrapped the remnant about her chest and tied it in a knot. Just as she was thinking what an odd-looking bikini top she had fashioned, she realized she was settling down into the mud, which now reached to her knees.

"Help! I'm sinking!" she pleaded, pulling one leg out of the slime, while the smell of rotting vegetation gagged her.

"Don't be silly. Just float through the reeds."

"I can't. They're grabbing my legs."

"Here," he said, and she saw his hand two inches from her nose.

She grasped it and pulled violently. He plunged forward and splashed near her in the muck, sending sticky globs to cover her face and hair. With muddy water swirling about their waists, they sat staring at each other, then broke out laughing.

"I didn't mean to dunk you," she said. The sun, dappling through the willow leaves, was tracing copper and flaxen highlights in his hair and his aristocratic face glowed with amusement.

"I know. The bank gave way and I lost my footing." His eyebrow rose as he added, "You're even prettier than I had pictured you. I expect that when you're cleaned up you're a real beauty. The color of your mud pack, though, does nothing for your complexion and detracts from those incredible violet eyes of yours. I think peach-colored makeup would be more becoming than the brown you're wearing, don't you agree?"

Automatically, her hands swiped over her cheeks. "Stop

being childish," she chided, but couldn't keep from smiling.

"I'll be happy to act like a man. How old are you?" he asked with a lopsided grin.

"You're not supposed to ask a woman her age."

"I'm twenty-eight, and you must be very young or very old if you won't tell me. That complicates matters."

"I'll not be staying in your country long enough for any matters to be complicated."

"I'll have to see what I can do to make you change your mind," Jacques said, grasping her hand firmly and pulling her away from the reeds, back to where the bottom of the pond was sandy. "Come on, we won't solve your present problem sitting in this muck arguing."

Janine leaned forward in the clear water and washed her face and rubbed her short hair vigorously while Jacques ran his hands across his chest, trying to clean his shirt.

"This is a novel way to do the laundry," he said, scrubbing his clothes.

"And to shampoo hair," she said, thinking his gray eyes were the color of the sky just before dawn.

"But it's fun, don't you think?"

"Personally, I wouldn't have chosen this particular type of entertainment," she replied. His leg accidentally touched hers and she suddenly became more conscious of her near nudity.

His gaze dived underwater. "I have to agree there are more enjoyable diversions. I'm game, if you are." He reached for her shoulder, let his hand linger there a moment, then plucked off a leaf.

The searching expression on the face of this spectacular-looking man, his caressing voice, and the butterfly touch of his fingers raised goosebumps all over her. Avoiding his eyes, which were now studying her with appreciation and amusement, she stated with all the coolness she could muster, "I'm not game. Forget it."

As she swam toward the shallows, foaming the still pond with her choppy crawl, she didn't hear his reply. She kneeled on the sand near the shore, keeping herself under water from the waist down.

The chestnut stallion nibbled wild oats in the shade of an ancient oak tree while Heidi lay in the grass chewing on the other half of the red sundress. She had stopped barking long ago.

"You sure were a big help, you old mutt. All you did was tear up my clothes and now you're using them for a snack."

"Better your clothes than your admirers," Jacques said, stepping onto the bank and scratching behind the dog's ears. He pulled off his boots and let the water run out.

Janine watched him remove his socks and shirt, wring them out, and spread them over a tangle of honeysuckle to dry. His shoulders were broad and his muscles rippled with each movement. A mat of blond hair, darkened by the water, curled on his chest, arrowed down his flat abdomen, and disappeared below his belt. Her eyes grew wide and she turned away, hoping he'd let his riding britches dry in place.

"Don't worry, I won't strip." He smiled, and she crossed her hands in her lap. Her transparent bikini briefs provided no cover at all.

"How am I going to get home?" she asked as her gaze measured his six-foot frame.

"You have several choices." Counting on his fingers, he began offering solutions. "I'll lend you Max and you can thrill the villagers by riding into Orpe Le Petit like Lady Godiva."

"Please be serious."

"You're right. That wouldn't do. Your hair's so short that it doesn't even cover your neck. All right then, wait till my shirt is dry and wear it like a minidress. They'll think that's the latest American fashion. Or you might just wait here and let me fetch a dress for you. Actually, I'd be back in less than half an hour with my car and your clothes."

She saw that he had stopped joking and was trying to be helpful. "What time is it?" she asked. She had to know before making her decision. If she could get to her bedroom before her relatives closed their café and came home for lunch, she wouldn't have to explain her misadventure and listen to their scolding. Laure especially was a terrible nag and seemed unable to comprehend that Janine didn't want to adhere to a meal schedule that limited her movements. Having kept her promise of some travel articles to the editor of the *Johnson County Gazette*, a suburban daily to which she had contributed freelance features during the past couple of years, Janine intended to continue exploring and writing.

Jacques looked at his watch, still functioning after the dip. "It's a quarter to one. Do you have a pressing engagement?" he joked.

"Monsieur Laurent, if I don't reach home within fifteen minutes, I'll be in trouble."

"Let's dispense with the formalities, shall we? My name is Jacques," he said, handing her his damp shirt.

Slipping on the shirt, she pulled it down as she stood up in the water. It provided a bit more cover than she had expected. She joined him on the bank.

"Very fetching," he remarked, inclining his head to study the effect.

His gray eyes traveled up her shapely, tanned legs to her softly rounded hips and breasts. Deftly she removed the wet piece of sundress and dropped it in the grass. Conscious that her erect nipples pressed revealingly against the damp, white knit fabric, she crossed her arms over her chest. "You're embarrassing me, Jacques. Can't you see that I'm at a disadvantage?"

"I'm sorry. Perhaps I'm being insensitive. It's just that our chance encounter was such an unexpected treat and I still can't believe my luck. Because of the heat, I almost didn't ride today, and if I hadn't we might never have met."

She smiled up at him. "Yes. But I really should hurry now."

"Come on, I'll take you home," he said grudgingly, and she knew he wanted her to stay. He put on his wet socks and boots and she stepped into her sandals.

Max held perfectly still while Jacques cupped his hands and boosted her up. Joining her, he placed his left arm around her waist, holding the bridle in his right hand. The riding crop in his left hand lay along her thigh, its tip tickling her ankle. Jacques's bare chest felt warm and hard and supple against her back.

"You'll have to tell me who you are and where you live, won't you?" His chin touched her ear.

His breath in her hair, his body molded to hers, and his arm with its golden hairs encircling her made Janine forget for a moment where she was and what she was about. She leaned her head back against his shoulder while Max pranced and Heidi circled about his hooves. Janine sighed.

"Have you changed your mind about going home?" His thumb caressed her waist, and the huskiness of his voice sent a wave of heat through her while the desire to turn her head and look into the depths of his eyes nearly overwhelmed her.

She swallowed and leaned forward, surprised at the responses her body was making as if all connections with her will and her mind had been severed. She had never felt so physically drawn to a man before in her life and she felt awash in emotion, while tingling sensations crept across her skin. The yellow weeds and buttercups along the path were like a bower inviting them to stretch full length in each other's arms. Shaking her head, she replied as coolly as she could manage, "No, I haven't. Let's go."

"Where to, mystery girl?"

She remembered that he didn't know who she was because she had never answered his question, overcome by his nearness. "I'm Janine Heerlen, Monsieur and Madame Pierre Heerlen's niece. If you turn right at the end of the lane, we're just a mile from their house."

"I know where they live, Janine." On his lips, her name sounded like a caress. He tightened his grip about her waist and the horse broke into a gallop while the Doberman, teeth clamped firmly about the red rubber ball, followed at a graceful lope.

Soon they were racing along the road, which was lined by houses that sat behind closed shutters on wooded lots dotted with flower beds. For a moment Janine thought that if the principal of the high school where she was going to teach in the fall could see her now, he would surely revoke her contract, but then the rippling motion of the stallion's muscles and Jacques's face so close to hers made her feel drunk with the joy of being alive. All she wanted was for the mad gallop to last forever.

But in a few minutes Jacques reined in the horse before the Heerlens' house. "It's almost one o'clock," he said and helped her dismount. For a moment he held her hand in his firm grip and she felt like a small bird captured in his grasp.

He tightened his jaw and his gray eyes were like steel blades when he said in a low, controlled voice, "I hope you appreciate the willpower I have summoned not to scoop you back up and spirit you away."

She stepped back and held on to the gate while a thrill ran through her. Was it fear or desire that he would follow his words with action? And what if he was only teasing her and after he rode away she never saw him again? This was sheer idiocy, she chided herself. He was so handsome and wealthy that his life was probably teaming with love-struck women willing to spend a few passionate hours with him without expecting a promise or a commitment. But she would never be one of them.

"If you were to try that trick, I promise I wouldn't behave like a sack of potatoes and let you cart me away in silence. Thanks for the ride," she said, looking up at him and stretching the shirt down as far as it would go while his eyebrows quirked in amusement. She should have gone in now, but she stood rooted to the spot.

"I would never have compared you to a sack of potatoes. You're curvy, not lumpy. I'm really sorry about your dress." Waving his crop, he added, "I'll see you soon." Flicking the bridle across the magnificent animal's neck, he trotted down the road. In a moment, all that remained of his presence was the echo of hoofbeats. Had she imagined the encounter? His body had been solid enough and she could still feel the heat of his chest on her slender back.

She unlatched the gate in the fence surrounding the attractive red-brick house surrounded by trees and flowers. Hearing a car turn into the road, Janine dashed into the house with Heidi at her heels and ran upstairs. Leaning against her bedroom door, she sighed with relief. She was safe. *Are you now?* an inner voice mocked her.

Within a few minutes she had slipped into a yellow T-shirt and denim culottes and was sitting at lunch with Laure and Pierre, grateful for the breeze that cooled her face and ruffled her hair, sending a dark wisp to tickle her temple. According to Pierre, the heat wave was very unusual for Belgium, which was famous for its cool, rainy summers.

"Would you like a little more salad, Janine?" Pierre asked as he carved the roast. He looked tired, he had been working since seven o'clock.

"Yes, please," she replied, smiling into his soft brown eyes. She finished the salad, then tackled the roast. She had not realized how hungry she was.

"I go to Nivelle especially to buy fresh vegetables. Our garden is overrun by weeds," Laure said, pursing her lips and pushing her steel-rimmed spectacles up on her nose. Then she started on a stream of complaints about Henriette and Maurice Blanchard, the elderly couple who came in every day and whose responsibility it was to take care of house and grounds.

Janine glanced over the L-shaped dining room and living room combination. The waxed surface of the low coffee table reflected the yellow roses in a pewter bowl, and the sheer curtains looked newly laundered. There wasn't a speck of dust anywhere. Janine wanted to steer the conversation to Jacques Laurent, but she hesitated because the preceding day her aunt had left her with the impression that she detested him. Perhaps he was in the habit of visiting their café, and she intended to go there this evening. Suddenly she realized that he hadn't asked to see her again. He'd just said he'd see her soon. What if he waited till she had left for Paris?

After a dessert of strawberries and cream, Janine helped Laure clear the table. The housekeeper would wash the dishes later.

Following their usual routine, Pierre went to rest and Laure sat at the dining-room table playing solitaire while Janine kept her company. The shuffling of the cards was the only noise in the quiet house.

Laure played game after game and talked about Janine's parents' fatal car accident the previous year, the café, the Blanchards, and a palm-oil plantation Grandfather Heerlen had owned in the Belgian Congo. Time and again she used the expression *beaucoup d'argent*. It was odd how she could place a monetary value on everything.

Janine tuned her out and thought about her meeting with Jacques. At a lull in the monologue, she asked, "Aunt Laure, didn't you tell me you lease the café from Jacques Laurent?"

"Yes. He owns the building, just as he owns Les Alouettes, the estate that used to belong to your family." Laure pursed her lips, sending spidery lines from her mouth to her nose.

"I believe I was there today during my walk with Heidi."

Laure sighed. "The Heerlens lost Les Alouettes a long time ago, during the Depression, and you shouldn't have trespassed. It's not ours any longer. That's the way the world turns. The rich get richer and the poor get poorer. Now the rumor is that Monsieur Laurent is planning to tear down our café and build an automobile-repair shop there. You've got to be ruthless and grasping to make it, I always say, and he and his family could give lessons to the devil himself." She slammed the queen of spades on the king of hearts and continued, "If our family hadn't lost everything and gone steadily downhill, your father wouldn't have abandoned his homeland and emigrated to a foreign country."

"But he loved his job. He used to say that being a history

professor was all he had ever wanted to be." But she remembered that Guy Heerlen had often remarked that he was like a man without a country. The United States had been good to him, but it wasn't really his home and neither was Belgium any longer. She had always thought she would never let that happen to her. America was her home and this sentimental trip to see her paternal roots had been a mistake.

Ignoring the remark, Laure continued, "And you. As pretty as you are, by now you should have made a good marriage instead of having to make your own living. You'll never have servants to do your bidding, or give lavish parties, or drive expensive sportscars." She pushed her spectacles up on her nose and peered at her niece, shaking her head. Her hair, dyed a harsh reddish brown, made her look much older than her fifty years.

Running her hand through her curls, Janine remembered her lovely split-level home awaiting her return, with her white Buick Skylark parked in the double garage, and thought that she had never felt deprived. If she hadn't known that Pierre and Laure were comfortable and could retire if they wished, she might have felt sorry for her aunt. As it was, it appeared to her that Laure was the one who envied the luxuries she claimed to wish for her niece.

"I'm quite satisifed with my life, Aunt Laure," Janine said, pushing back her chair. "I think I'll go take a nap now. The walk and the heat made me more tired than I expected."

"You'll come to the café after a bit, won't you? You promised you'd help out, and besides, we've talked about you so much to all our customers that they want to meet you. Everyone was disappointed when you didn't show up yesterday." The solitaire wasn't coming out right and Laure started moving cards about without any regard for the rules.

"Don't worry, I'll come this evening," Janine replied and ran upstairs.

That afternoon she dreamed she was perched in a sway-

ing palm tree in a jungle clearing, while Jacques, on a
winged horse, hovered above and tried to pull her up. But
their hands wouldn't reach and he dissolved in the clouds.
Then Janine noticed that the trees dripped a clear golden
oil till the entire clearing became a pool of melted gold. The
golden lake slowly turned to quicksilver, and Laure, standing on the shore with a long-handled ladle, scooped the silvery oil into huge drums and chanted, *"Beaucoup
d'argent, beaucoup d'argent."*

When she woke up, the rays of the setting sun reflecting
from the wardrobe mirror filled the room with a rosy light.
Doves on the roof and in the chestnut tree outside the
window cooed their mating call and the scent of roses mingled with that of new-mown grass.

Janine changed into a lavender shirtwaist dress that
enhanced the violet color of her eyes and slipped into a pair
of high-heeled bone pumps. While she washed her face and
applied a light dusting of powder and lip gloss, she found
herself hoping that Jacques would come to the café this
evening.

Walking toward the village, she passed a tiny walled
graveyard with marble monuments and family vaults
crowded together, along weedy graveled paths. Then she
took the road that forked by an old farmhouse where a
manure pile was heaped in the middle of the central courtyard. Farm smells were the same the world over, she
thought as she waved a fly away from her face.

In five minutes she was in sight of the cobblestoned village square, but had to stop at the lowered barrier of the
railroad crossing. By the barrier was a tiny, whitewashed
station surrounded by pink geraniums. On the platform,
looking east toward the rumble of the oncoming train, was
a railroad employee in a billed cap and a dark blue uniform
with brass buttons. Pierre had told her that Brussels was
just a fifteen-minute train ride away and she decided that
tomorrow she'd go to the capital and spend the day. She
particularly wanted to visit the Grand' Place, and her
impressions would provide material for an interesting arti-

cle. Laure would have to understand that she couldn't return home for lunch.

The train passed with a whoosh of hot air. When the barrier was raised, Janine crossed the tracks and walked on to the Heerlens' café. CAFÉ CENTRAL was painted in gold letters across a large plate-glass window and a red Jaguar was parked outside.

As she opened the door, a heavy, fruity odor of wine and malt greeted her and she realized that the café was actually a family-type bar. With an elbow on the bar and a pint of beer in his hand, Jacques, in a blue suit that enhanced the flaxen streaks in his burnished hair, smiled at Janine and raked his gray eyes over her slender body. The sun, slanting through the window and reflecting off the whitewashed walls, seemed to envelop him in brightness.

Two

"Janine, I'd like you to meet Monsieur Jacques Laurent," said Pierre, who had been drawing draft beer behind the bar.

Shaking her hand, Jacques bowed slightly while a flicker of amusement played in his gray eyes and his lips quirked in a smile. "It's a pleasure to make your acquaintance, mademoiselle." His touch made her think of their parting a few hours before, when she had feared she would never see him again. She should have known he wouldn't let that happen. It had been evident from the very beginning that he was as attracted to her as she was to him.

Without giving her time to reply, Pierre whisked her away and introduced her to the other men and women crowding the booths and tables.

The café was like an oasis in the quiet village and within minutes more customers came in as the commuter train from Brussels arrived. Janine was presented to each newcomer, but all she was conscious of was Jacques's gaze, continually following her.

Patting her hair in place, Laure entered the café from a door at the rear, and at the sight of Jacques Laurent pasted a tight smile on her face. She turned to Marie Louise, a buxom, brown-haired girl in her middle twenties who, in her yellow peasant blouse and flowered dirndl skirt, flitted about the tables like a bright-feathered bird. "Janine said she'd give us a hand when we're busy," she said to the waitress.

Marie Louise handed Janine a tray of foaming steins and smiled. "These are for the two couples in the far booth. I'll be happy for the help." Then she whirled about, and in picking up a cup of coffee and a glass of grenadine for a thin, blond woman sitting at a small table with a toddler, she bumped into Janine. The tray in Janine's hands slipped and a glass tipped over, spilling beer onto the floor.

Jacques jumped back and looked at the liquid beading one of his highly polished black shoes. With a grin he said, "Every time we meet, you either dunk or sprinkle me. Are you trying to wash away my sins?"

"Even sticking your head under the beer spigot wouldn't accomplish that." She placed another glass of beer on the tray.

"I can think of more pleasurable ways, even though you'd probably think that what I have in mind would cast me deeper into perdition."

"Perhaps a cold shower would be a good solution for you." She started to walk away, but his voice, low and urgent, detained her.

"How long are you going to postpone the inevitable?"

"Nothing is inevitable and I am not a fatalist."

"What I meant was, when are you going to stop playing barmaid and leave? Wouldn't you rather talk to me without an audience?"

"Soon," she answered quickly. Laure had been staring from Jacques to Janine without understanding. He was addressing her in English and she automatically replied in the same language, but now she was becoming acutely aware of the rudeness of their maneuver.

"That's a relief. When you first walked in, the sun shined right through your skirt and outlined your legs. In their transparent lilac cover they were even more enticing than when I saw them this morning completely unveiled. I thought Eros had shot me through the heart with one of his arrows, then I realized it was your aunt shooting daggers through me with her eyes." He clutched his chest and leaned forward across the bar.

"Are you all right, Monsieur Laurent?" Pierre asked, his voice full of concern.

"Yes, of course. It's just that my English is not nearly as fluent as mademoiselle's, and it's such a strain for me to understand the nuances of her conversation."

Janine hid a smile and finally delivered the beer to the two couples in the far booth.

During the next half-hour, she was so busy that she hardly had time to think. Fortunately, that helped her overcome her embarrassment at her new role of barmaid. She would have liked to talk to Jacques, who, standing at the bar, nursed his beer and smiled at her each time their eyes met. When the crowd thinned and only four cardplayers were left, Marie Louise ran about, scrubbing the counter and tables and emptying ashtrays.

Janine turned to her uncle and said, "I think I'll leave now, if you don't need me anymore."

"Sure, child, run along, and thanks for the help," Pierre said.

"If you wait another half an hour, you can ride home with us," Laure interjected.

"Mademoiselle is going to Brussels with me," Jacques said firmly, and taking Janine by the arm he headed toward the door.

"It's after eight o'clock. Too late to be running around." Laure peered from one to the other with pinched lips.

Pierre winked at Janine and, ignoring his wife's frown, said, "You'll never see Brussels at night with us. Have a good time."

"Good night," Janine called to her relatives as Jacques propelled her out the door and into the red Jaguar.

The thought of seeing Brussels at night escorted by Jacques Laurent filled Janine with delight. He avoided the autoroute and drove through the countryside along the two-lane highway that cut knifelike through Orpe Le Petit,

Lillois, and Waterloo. The small towns seemed to be asleep behind closed green shutters. Now that they were finally alone with the entire evening before them, their silence seemed to pull them closer, and Janine inhaled deeply the fragrance of the summer night. Every time she looked at Jacques, he glanced at her as if drawn by her thoughts. She felt as if a magnetic force joined them together as they sped through the night.

"I'm anything but timid," Jacques said, "however, I'm really not willing to subject myself to your aunt's antagonism again. I felt as if she thought I meant to steal her favorite bottle of Chateau de Rothschild."

"Aren't you exaggerating?" Janine laughed at being compared to a vintage wine. "And shouldn't you rather compare me to a jug of Mogen-David? That's what my friends and I like to drink with 7-Up in the summer. It's called a wine cooler."

Jacques stared at her. "Please! I see I'll have to educate your palate." Continuing his previous train of thought, he said, "I should have made a date with you, but you were in such a hurry. Then, when I tried to call you, I discovered your relatives have an unlisted number, so my only recourse was to come to the café. I didn't know it was going to be so difficult to tear you away from there."

They had reached Brussels, where residential and business areas alternated with long stretches of parkland and forests. Janine saw a sliver of moonlight shimmer on a small lake nestled among trees. "How lovely," she said.

"Yes, you are, dressed or otherwise." He chuckled.

"I meant the lake."

"And I can think of nothing but you. However, if you want a tour of the city, that's the Lake of the Drowned Children and I'll not allow you to swim there. It's full of algae," Jacques teased.

Janine sighed, determined not to spoil the evening. Was he ever going to let her forget her embarrassment at the pond? She averted her head so he couldn't see her face, then a secret smile dimpled her cheeks. If she hadn't acted unconventionally, she might not have met him.

As they drove between rows of two- and three-story row houses, Janine had the feeling that staid burghers of old were peering through lorgnettes at the bustle of the present century. The steeply-pitched roofs, the high narrow windows, and the carved lintels, cornices and moldings gave the buildings a rather forbidding, typically northern European flavor which was lightened by window boxes spilling over with geraniums and petunias.

"Why are all street signs and traffic directions in both French and Flemish?" she asked, puzzled. Brussels was in the heart of French-speaking Brabant.

He looked as if his mind was someplace else when he replied, "There's so much animosity between the Walloons and Flemish sharing this small nation that the government tries to appease both groups."

Now they were on the Avenue Louise, where six lanes of heavy traffic gave the impression of rush hour in Kansas City, and when Jacques stopped at a light before crossing the Boulevard de Waterloo, he said, "It's strange how the same event can affect two persons so differently. For me, our encounter was charming. I came upon a water nymph hiding among the branches of a willow tree. The heat of the sun, the song of the birds, and the scent of mint and honeysuckle completed the picture of a perfect summer day. I felt connected to all my male ancestors, as if they were looking at the world through my eyes, feeling with my body." He reached for her hand and imprisoned it in his own. At his touch, an aching awareness of his nearness filled her and she responded to the gentle pressure of his fingers. "Your femininity and your vulnerability were like a prodding, or more nearly an uncontrollable urge, to perpetuate myself. I could visualize my descendants and my own immortality."

Janine was filled with sudden fear and withdrew her hand. Was he suggesting that there at the pond he had wanted to give her a child? Ever since she had met him her attraction for him had been unmistakable, but he was moving much too fast. She forced herself to quip, "The DNA in your cells tried to overwhelm your reason. I know that civilization is only a veneer on our biological instincts, but no one has ever told me that they were overwhelmed by their genetic code and chemical composition."

"But wasn't the chemistry right for you?"

"Jacques, you're scaring me and making me very uncomfortable."

His voice had been soft, almost as if he were musing to himself. Now he added with cool charm, "I'm sorry that for you our meeting was only an embarrassment."

Looking down at her hand, still warm from his touch, Janine murmured, "It was more than just that."

"I'm glad you're willing to admit that the sexual urge is the most powerful force in the world."

"Jacques, I want you to stop this kind of conversation right now."

"You're afraid of your own feelings, but denying them won't make them go away. When you looked away from me as I was teasing you about swimming in the lake, I thought that earlier in the day perhaps I had misread your body language, even though I had always thought that it was the same all over the world," he said, backing his Jaguar into a spot just vacated by a white Ford on the Rue de L'Etuve. Helping her out of the car and acting as if their exchange was completely forgotten, he remarked, "I wasn't going to take you out of the way to show you the Manneken Pis, especially since I've found Americans to be rather prudish, but it's right across the street."

She didn't like his comment and wanted to ask him how he would feel if she were to make the same type of remark about his countrymen. Instead, she held her head higher and said, "I've seen pictures of it. There's also one very similar on the Country Club Plaza in Kansas City."

"A charming city, that, full of friendly people, and you're their most enticing prototype," he said, and her heart skipped a beat as she realized that if he had visited there before, perhaps he would visit there again once she returned home.

She moved to the railing among a group of English tourists and gazed at the small bronze statue of a little boy squirting water into a fountain. "I understand that the fortunes of the 'Oldest Inhabitant of Brussels' are linked to the fortunes of the city."

"That's the legend, and I wish I knew how to cast a spell and link your fortunes to mine," he replied, taking her arm as they walked away.

The firm but gentle grip of Jacques's fingers on her elbow sent a tingle through Janine and she felt as if each nerve ending had been sensitized by his touch. She saw him glanced down at her and she squeezed his hand between her elbow and her waist. She looked at the displays in shop windows but soon found that she could not focus on anything. All her awareness was concentrated on his presence at her side.

When they entered the famous Grand' Place, Janine stood transfixed in admiration of the immense flagstoned marketplace surrounded by buildings of different heights, which created a highly irregular skyline. Varicolored floodlights played their part in the spectacle, enhancing the opulence of the medieval square.

"This is incredible," Janine murmured, looking from the Gothic palace that housed the City Museum to the Hotel de Ville with its famous Lion Stairway.

"And this morning you were talking about leaving. I told you I'd try to talk you out of it. If you enjoy the architecture of Belgium, perhaps you'll also learn to appreciate that of one of its inhabitants."

Laughing, she gave him a brief, encompassing glance and said, "I do." Looking at the facades of the surrounding buildings, which were so ornate as to seem almost theatrical, she pointed to an equestrian statue and said, "I think that's a gorgeous knight."

"I believe I can compete for your affections against

Charles of Lorraine. I might not have the power he used to wield, but he is no more, while I'm very much alive."

Janine thought there was no denying that. She could feel the heat of his body next to hers. "I'd planned to stay in Belgium another week or so, but I'm not at ease where I am."

"Is your room not comfortable?"

"My room's all right, although I wish there were screens on the windows."

"Screens are a big boon, but there are compensations. I love the window in my bedroom. It looks into the walled garden and a huge wisteria vine circles it completely. Right now the vine is in bloom and the scent is so delicate. Will you let me show it to you? I think it might make you forget all about American conveniences."

"No, Jacques. Your window and your bedroom are not part of my European tour." She moved away from him. "Suddenly I have the feeling that when you were in Kansas City you haunted the bars and nightclubs of Westport, and that your knowledge of American women is what you gathered from those surroundings." She had been in that area only once and had been repelled by the manner in which men and women eyed one another, just as if they were shopping at a meat market.

"Yes, I was there, and it's a very lively place. I admire the freedom of American women. They're just as free as the Scandinavians."

"If you're assuming I'm like that, you're making a mistake," she said, holding herself stiffly. She looked at the artistically scrolled stone, marble, and gilt surfaces that competed for attention with banners waving in the wind. The flags were a symphony of colors and symbols.

Following her eyes, Jacques explained that the buildings had been erected in ancient times as guildhouses and the banners were those of the various guilds. Then he stopped abruptly and turned her to face him. "I keep feeling that if I take a wrong step you'll disappear among the silos and windmills of Kansas and I'll never find you again. Please give us a chance to know each other better. If you don't like living at the Heerlens', come and stay at my chateau. You'll be free to come and go as you please."

"I couldn't do that," she said. Things were moving too fast for her. She had just met him this morning and he was already trying to have her move into his place.

"Janine, you know I wouldn't press my attentions on you. I think this morning should have reassured you."

She smiled and nodded. "You could have grabbed me if you had wanted to and no one would have heard me if I had screamed."

Jacques laughed. "Make no mistake. I did want to, as you so quaintly put it, 'grab you,' but that's just not my style. I meant what I said, though, and it's not quite as it sounds. My stepmother and her niece, Monette, are spending a month at the chateau and my father'll be there in a few days, as soon as he returns from England. Monette is nineteen years old and I know you would enjoy meeting her." Seeing her frown, he said, "I'm only trying to reassure you, and I can't understand why you're so determined to discount what's happening between us."

"I'm not discounting anything. I only want you to slow down. When you put so much pressure on, I feel like running from you. If you tell me how to find your place, I promise that at least I'll come to see you. But I'm afraid I can't accept your invitation to stay. My relatives' feelings would really be hurt." Still, the thought of living under the same roof with him lingered in her mind and her planned trip to Paris receded in the distance. What would it be like to see him every day and to be alone with him? That was exactly what she wanted. Overwhelmed by the realization of her feelings, she looked down at the ancient flagstones and slowed her pace while Jacques explained to her where the chateau was located, and she was surprised to learn it was less than two miles from the Heerlens'.

Soon he turned the conversation back to his offer of hospitality. "I hope you aren't afraid I'll waylay you on a country lane and swoop you up on my stallion. Unfortunately, the

ays when the master could exercise his *droit du seigneur*
re no more. Taking a woman's virginity on her wedding
ight is illegal. You'll be safe under my roof."

Remembering the feel of his naked chest against her
ody as they galloped through the midday heat, she
odded, unable to speak, and the laughter at his banter
ied in her throat.

"I've thought of nothing but you since this morning," he
aid, taking her chin in his hand.

His touch was as soft as a dove's wing and his gray eyes
lumbed her violet depths and traveled to her mouth. Her
ps parted and she closed her eyes while the hum of the
rowd seemed to enclose them in a secret place where the
ind stopped functioning and only the body dictated its
esires. She was a caldron of emotions and feelings
wirling about unchecked. His finger touched her lips and
e murmured, "Not here, *petite amie.*"

Her heavy lids flew open and, trying to focus her eyes, she
ulled away, realizing how much she had wanted his kiss.
o regain her composure, she looked about her and
erooted herself in her surroundings. Seeing a banner with
two-headed falcon on a red field, she said, surprised at
ne hoarseness of her voice, "Perhaps I could start my arti-
le with: 'In the heart of ancient Brussels is the famous
rand' Place, a monument to Belgian craftsmen and mer-
hants.' I do wish I had brought my camera, though."

"Photography's my father's hobby," Jacques replied.
When you come to my place, you can choose any photo-
raph you wish." He had seen her embarrassment and was
rying to put her at ease.

For a while they strolled in silence and Janine tried to
ok at the sights, but all she could see was Jacques's aris-
ocratic hand with its long, tapering fingers grasping her
ghtly by the elbow. The fine blond hairs on the back of his
and made her think of the muscles rippling on his chest
hen he had removed his shirt at the pond, and it was
early impossible to distract herself from his touch. She
ooked at a little boy licking a chocolate ice cream cone.

"What flavor would you like?" Jacques asked with an amused smile.

"Strawberry," she replied quickly. "But first let me look in these shops a moment."

He followed her as she looked in the windows. Janine admired the Belgian handicrafts and commented, "Everything's terribly expensive, or else I'm mixed up on the rate of exchange."

Jacques teased, "Let me know what appeals to you and I'll satisfy your every whim. Would you like one of those lace tablecloths from Bruges, or some engraved crystal from the Val Saint Lambert? Or perhaps that white silk neglige trimmed in ermine? I can picture you letting it drop from your shoulders onto the floor and standing there waiting for me, like Venus surrounded by seafoam."

He looked at her hungrily and she felt as if he were stripping away her clothes. She hurried up the steps of another shop and he joined her.

Standing before the window, their reflections looked back at them from the spotless glass. His tall, fair figure provided a foil for her petite, dark beauty and her violet eyes met his smoky glance. Then she looked down and saw a delicate crystal bud vase with the etched figure of a huntress wearing a short tunic and carrying a bow and quiver, and she imagined she could smell the perfume of the deep carmine rosebud it held.

They rejoined the crowd on the pavement. Jacques guided her to a sidewalk café and sipped coffee while she ate ice cream. His eyes followed each spoonful to her mouth and lingered there.

She chattered about herself, trying to keep silences from developing. As long as she talked, she could almost ignore his knee pressed against hers under the table and the eyes that seemed to want to devour her lips. Jacques appeared interested in all the details of her life, and when he volunteered to talk about himself, she was surprised to discover that he had returned from the United States only two weeks before. On learning that, in partnership with Monsieur

Fronville, a neighbor, Jacques had bought a vineyard in Missouri, less than twenty miles from her suburban Kansas home. Janine was filled with happiness at the thought that she would surely see him again once she returned home. It seemed to her as if somehow her trip to Belgium had been fated.

"I think my editor would be very interested in a feature article about your American enterprise, and it would be a fun piece to write. Will you give me an interview?"

"I don't like publicity." She felt very disappointed. If she decided to stay in Belgium a few days longer, perhaps she could interview Monsieur Fronville and gather the information she would need. Jacques changed the subject. "Do you have a city map of Brussels?" he asked, leaning back in his chair. "It'd be useful if you want to explore on your own."

"I really need one." His knee had moved away and she wondered if he had resented her request.

"If you don't mind being left alone for a few minutes, I'll buy it for you."

She reached in her purse to give him the money, but he had already disappeared in the crowd. She placed fifty francs by his cup.

Then Jacques returned and placed on the table the bud vase she had admired before. The red rose smelled as sweet as Janine had imagined.

"Oh!" she said, clasping her hands in wonder at the beauty of the vase and the rose. Then she remembered the outlandish price. He would have to return it.

"Do you like it?" An expectant smile played on his lips.

"I couldn't possibly accept it." She slid the vase toward him. "Please take it back." She saw his jaws clench and knew she had hurt his feelings.

He took the city map from his pocket and placed it on her purse, then saw the money by his coffee cup. "What's this for?"

"The map."

He toyed with the coins. "All right, I'll make a deal with

you, Janine. I'll let you pay for the map if you'll accept the vase."

"But you mustn't buy me presents. It's not proper."

"Most proper things are rather dull, don't you agree?" An ironic smile quirked his mouth, and the cleft in his chin was so attractive that Janine wanted to touch it. "By accepting the vase you'll assure me that you've forgiven me for the destruction of your sundress."

"But Heidi was just as responsible."

"Unfortunately, Heidi cannot make amends." He covered her hand with his and she left it nestled there, warm and trembling. Pointing to the huntress delicately etched on the crystal, he murmured, his voice so deep and mellow that a shiver ran down her spine, "I told you at the pond about the goddess Artemis, that beautiful, cruel figure of myth who turned the unwary prince into a stag. You see, Actaeon chanced unaware upon her as she prepared to bathe, and you'd think she'd have taken into account the fact that he was hunting in the forest and by nature was not a peeping Tom. But no. That maiden goddess of the moon and the hunt was cruel and unyielding." His face was serious, but his choice of words left no doubt that he was teasing.

"Oh, Jacques." She laughed. If he was comparing her to Artemis, he was wrong in thinking she was unyielding. She so much wanted to feel his arms around her that it was difficult to concentrate on his banter.

"His own hunting dogs tore him limb from limb, just as your Doberman was trying to do to me." His gray eyes traveled to her mouth and lingered there.

She licked her lips, then shook her head and said, "You're scrambling your story. The dog was mine, not yours, and if I recall, she was perfectly content to let you scratch her ears. You're also mixing your metaphors. Peeping Tom was struck blind when he looked upon Lady Godiva. He doesn't belong in the legend of Artemis and Actaeon."

"I'll concede that. But you have to agree that I didn't actually see you at your bath, either." His thumb caressed her wrist and his knee pressed hers. The smile had disappeared from his lips.

Beginning to feel uncomfortable, she said, "I was swimming. Stop saying I was taking a bath."

"Perhaps my subconscious is prompting my choice of words. I would love to wash your back."

Pointing to the vase, she asked, "Is this supposed to be an eternal reminder of my foolishness?"

Gently he slid the vase toward her. "No. It's to remind you of my admiration for your beauty, and in accepting it you'll let me know my attentions are not unwelcome."

At his gallantry, Janine felt that a further refusal would be boorish. "Thank you so much, Jacques. I'll always treasure it. It'll remind me of . . ." She had wanted to say *you*, but corrected herself in time, "Belgium when I return home."

He kissed the palm of her hand, then closed her fingers around the kiss and looking into her eyes said, "I hope there'll be something warmer than crystal to remind you of your holiday."

A wave of heat traveled from her hand to her face and she felt as if she was losing control of her emotions. Perhaps it would be better if she returned home now, before she begged him to kiss her.

As if sensing her fear, Jacques leaned back in his chair and said, "Let's put the vase in the car, then we'll go to Chez Bernard. You'll enjoy it and I'll finally get to hold you in my arms as we dance."

"But I'm really not dressed to go to a nightclub," she said, looking down at her casual summer frock and thinking that fortunately she had worn high heels. Frowning, she wondered what kind of game she was playing. She wanted to dance with him, to feel his arms around her, his body close to hers, and she knew she didn't want to cut the outing short, yet she was trying to find reasons not to prolong the evening. Her words and her wishes were in constant contradiction. What was the matter with her? She had always been forthright, but now she found herself acting at odds with her desires. Could it be that she was terrified of her attraction for Jacques and didn't want to assume responsibility for her actions, letting him talk her into what she wanted all along so that she could hold herself blameless for whatever developed between them? The sudden awareness of this possibility made her decide to do her best to pull herself together.

"I love your lavender dress. You look so cool and dainty in it." He stood up and pulled back her chair while she marveled at his choice of adjectives. The first one certainly didn't fit. "It's time for you to have some dinner," he added.

"I'm not hungry," she said, picking up the vase. She inhaled the warm scent of the rose and stood up.

Walking at his side, she thought how handsome he looked in his European-cut blue suit. The silvery-gray stripes of his dark blue tie were the color of his eyes. Instead of reaching up to touch his white silk shirt, as she so much wanted to, she glanced at her watch and was surprised at how quickly the time had passed. It was nearly midnight. Would Laure be angry with her for staying out late? She dismissed the thought and wondered what she could do about her aunt's attempts to control her. She knew she wouldn't let Laure interfere with her seeing Jacques.

The cabaret was dim and crowded, but in a few moments a couple left and Jacques and Janine had a ringside seat by the tiny dance floor. Neither one of them wanted dinner and he ordered a bottle of champagne. Just as the waiter was filling their glasses, the multicolored spotlight encircled a young woman who had stepped onto the small stage. As she slung the strap of her guitar around her neck, she lifted her straight chestnut hair off her shoulders with a graceful motion that made the ample sleeve of her mauve gown slide up, revealing a shapely arm. She bowed at the smattering of applause and began to play. A hush fell. The singer's voice echoed in the room as she sang the plaintive words of an old French ballad. An Italian madrigal and an American folk song followed in quick succession.

The music, the champagne, and the subtle odor of women's perfume filled Janine with a sense of well-being, and she smiled at Jacques for sharing and enhancing the experience. Without him at her side, without the anticipation of dancing nestled in his arms and feeling his heartbeat responding to her own, this would have been just a dark little nightclub full of drinkers and smokers.

Jacques signaled to the waiter. There was a whispered conversation and money changed hands. Janine looked at Jacques questioningly, but he just raised his chin slightly, and when she followed his gaze she saw the waiter talking to the singer.

The young woman's voice was soft as a caress as she sang:

> O my luve's like a red, red rose
> That's newly sprung in June:
> O my luve's like the melodie
> That's sweetly played in tune!

The rest of the song enveloped Janine with tenderness, just like the arm Jacques had slipped about her waist. His fingers caressed the tender flesh under her upper arm and she leaned her head on his shoulder as she listened to the words of the Scottish ballad. She felt overwhelmed by his attentions. First he had given her a rose, then he had requested "A Red, Red Rose" be sung for her. She had never been courted in such a romantic way, and all his words were so loaded with his physical desire for her that she felt as if she were in the presence of a blast furnace ready to consume her.

When the song ended, the applause was deafening. Jacques's hand searched for hers and held it as they looked at each other, and Janine felt as if she were drowning in a misty sea. There was no need for him to tell her he wanted her. His eyes were speaking to her of unfathomable and unimagined delights. The spell was broken when the singer left the stage and immediately a combo began playing. Jacques stood up and Janine walked into his arms. Other couples crowded the dance floor, but Janine felt as if the two of them were alone. Cradled in his arms, she realized she had wanted to feel his hard male body pressed to hers ever since she had seen him on his magnificent chestnut stallion.

Gently he held her while his hand caressed her back with a circular, sensual motion, and as strange sensations traveled down her spine and legs, she wondered if she'd be able to stand up once he released her. With her forehead cradled in his neck, she drifted with the music, feeling a pulse beat in her temple. Was it his heart or her own rushing, pounding, filling the world? She wanted these moments to last forever.

When they returned to their table, she sipped her champagne and wondered what was happening to her. She had never felt so alive before, conscious of every nerve, every cell in her body, every fiber of her being.

His voice played a counterpoint to her sensations. "Are you thinking the same thoughts as I am?"

"Yes, Jacques." Her words caught in her throat and she tried to recapture her composure by saying, "It's nearly one o'clock. I must go home."

"Must you?"

She nodded, but wanted to beg, *Don't let me.* She had denied her desires once again, but there was no help for it. She couldn't give herself to him and in a few days return home never to see him again. There would have to be a serious commitment between them for her to abandon herself like that.

On the drive back to Orpe Le Petit, Janine's thoughts skittered to the dates she had had during the past few years. Each relationship had turned into friendship and never into love. The right chemistry had never happened. She had wondered if she was incapable of passion and if the right responses would somehow always be short-circuited. She knew better now. There was no short circuit in her attraction for Jacques. And it was alarming. Would she be able to keep to her decision to save herself for the man she would marry?

When they parked before the Heerlens' darkened house twenty minutes later, the moon was near the horizon and fireflies mirrored the stars in the black-velvet sky. The sweetness of the rose in the vase he'd bought for her melded with the masculine leather odor of the car's interior.

Jacques pulled her to him and clutched her to his chest, his fingers gripping her arms with an urgency that made her gasp, but she couldn't wait a second longer. She wanted his kiss. His lips traveled along her neck and he murmured huskily, "Janine, I want you unbearably. Please, don't hold back too long."

Then his mouth found hers and her lips parted like flower petals starved for the heat of the sun. His tongue was like the serpent in the Garden of Eden, tempting and seducing her. She moaned deep in her throat and her arms tightened around his neck. Her flesh begged him to take her, immediately, before she could think of the consequences. His breath in her ear sent shudders up and down her spine. Then suddenly the chirping of the crickets and the stillness of the night were shattered by Heidi's barking.

"Damn," he said under his breath and released her.

"She'll wake them up," Janine whispered. Clutching the bud vase, she dashed out of the car without waiting for his help.

Feeling as if her legs were made of dry sand, she stumbled, and Jacques was immediately at her side, supporting her. His voice was ragged as he pleaded, "Come to the chateau tomorrow."

Heidi's bark, loud and insistent, nearly drowned his words as they stood by the door. A light came on in the entryway.

"They're awake," she said, worried. On hearing her voice, Heidi quieted.

Jacques ignored her remark and insisted, "Tomorrow morning?"

"Not tomorrow. The following day. I'll call you." She had

decided that in the morning she would go to Brussels and check into a hotel, then she would telephone Jacques and they could see each other without Laure's objections.

"You'll telephone me tomorrow, though?" She nodded, and he had just turned her to face him when the front door opened a crack and Laure's harsh voice inquired, "Janine?"

"Yes, it's me," she answered. Then to Jacques she murmured, "You'd better go. I'll be in touch." His lips brushed the palm of her hand and he hurried away.

Standing by the door, she watched him stride to his car. His blue suit was a darker shade in the night, and the moon silvered his burnished-gold hair. She could hardly bear to let him go.

When her aunt opened the door wide, Janine walked into the house. Laure held her uncorseted body stiffly in her brown woolen robe, her eyes appearing naked without the metal-rimmed spectacles, and she opened and shut her mouth twice, as if unable to speak.

Janine's words tumbled out like a feeble attempt to stem the tide of the oncoming attack. "I'm sorry if I woke you up. I didn't realize Heidi was going to bark."

Rubbing his eyes, Pierre joined them in the foyer and said, "Come on, Laure, come to bed. Janine's home now and everything's all right."

Laure snorted. "You might think it is, but I certainly don't." She wheeled on her niece and pointed to the bud vase with the red rose, which Janine was cradling to her breast. "He thinks he can buy you with costly presents," she accused. As usual, Laure had used her favorite expression, *beaucoup d'argent*.

Pierre tried to soothe his wife. "Now, now Laure, I'm sure Janine fell in love with that pretty little vase and bought it herself."

Laure looked at her niece through narrowed eyes.

Acknowledging her uncle's attempt with a tight little smile, Janine answered, "No, Uncle Pierre, I didn't buy it." She wouldn't lie.

"I told you he's grasping and ruthless, and you . . . you practically spent the night with him! What do you expect to gain from it? Are you just defying me by throwing yourself at him or do you think he'll marry you?" Laure demanded.

"Aunt Laure, this conversation is ridiculous."

"Yes, Laure, please come to bed." Pierre placed an arm around his wife's shoulders.

She shook him off and hissed, "How do you expect me to sleep, Pierre? Jacques Laurent is trying to ruin our business and deprive us of our livelihood, and now this child, who's in our care, is ready to throw herself away on him. He'll use her and discard her, just as if she were a peasant girl."

"I'm not in your care and you're not responsible for me. Who ever said you were?" Janine took a step backward.

Laure turned to her. "You need to remember who you are, Janine, and stop disgracing our name. Your family's as honorable as his, even though he'll never acknowledge that. Don't let his charm blind you. He can switch it on and off at will. The two of you would have belonged to the same social class, and you'd be wealthy, too, if your grandfather hadn't lost his fortune. But now even Les Alouettes belongs to the Laurents, and Jacques would never, never marry you. You have nothing to offer him but your body, and if the vase is payment for it, you're selling yourself cheaply enough."

Janine could not control the trembling in her voice as she said, "You're insulting me and I don't have to listen to you. Even if this is your home and I'm your guest, you don't have the right to select my friends. I'll not stop seeing someone I like just because you hate him. It's quite clear you neither accept nor trust me, and I'm glad I've already made the decision to move out. Tomorrow I'm going into Brussels and check into a hotel."

Laure burst into sobs and hurried to her room.

Pierre walked with his niece to the foot of the stairs. "Your aunt is concerned about your welfare, but I'm afraid she got carried away. She's taking her responsibilities very seriously and has difficulty realizing that your upbringing has been very different from hers and that times have changed. Please stay; I'll have a talk with her."

"I'm sorry, Uncle Pierre, but my decision is firm. If you don't mind, I'll leave my suitcases here till I find a hotel room. I'll come back for them sometime tomorrow." Janine's knees were shaking and she clutched the banister. "I'm sorry if I woke you up, but that's the only apology I owe you or her."

"Please try to forgive her, Janine. She's of another generation and wants only to protect you." He kissed her on the forehead and added, "You'll have the house all to yourself tomorrow. We're going to a wedding in Bastogne and won't return till the following morning."

"Then I'll say goodbye now." She kissed her uncle on both cheeks and turned away.

The rose seemed to have lost its perfume as Janine walked up the steep staircase, her heels clicking on the bare polished wood. For a long time she tossed and turned in her bed without closing her eyes. Her aunt's agitated voice and her uncle's soothing tones drifting up to her room finally lapsed into silence. An owl hooted in the night and Janine remembered hearing the housekeeper say that it was a sign of bad luck.

Three

At ten o'clock the next night, Janine left Brussels without having found a vacant hotel room. A special session at NATO headquarters had crowded the city to the bursting limit. She resigned herself to spending another night at her relatives' and boarded the train back to Orpe Le Petit.

She arrived at the Heerlens' a little after midnight and walked silently across the lawn, her feet making silvery imprints in the dew-laden grass. The quarter moon cast a chill light over the darkened house and the concrete steps where she stood searching for her house key. A cricket chirped nearby and others answered, while from a hidden pond a chorus of frogs rasped their song. She felt a wave of nostalgia as she inhaled the air perfumed by the fragrance of nicotiana. The scent reminded her of home.

She removed her compact, wallet, and comb from her purse and shook it to see if she could locate the keys by their sound, but no jingling answered. Suddenly certain that she must have left them in her other purse, she walked around the house and tried to open the back door and all the windows she could reach, but, of course, they were locked. Realizing that there was no way to get into the house, she decided that the only solution was to accept Jacques's offer of hospitality.

But how could she show up at the chateau in the small

hours of the morning? Unless she wanted to curl up on the doorstep and wait for the Heerlens' arrival the following morning, she had no choice. Remembering Jacques's directions, she followed the road she had walked with Heidi two days before, and when she passed the turnoff that led to the pond with the weeping willow she knew the chateau was not much farther.

In the moonlight, the white petals of the hawthorns lining the country road floated down like a sprinkle of summer snow. Through breaks in the hedgerow she saw fields of grain and meadows where the dark shadows of cattle loomed like monoliths. Somehow the animals reassured her.

As she had done most of the day in her anxiety to find some accommodations, she thought of Jacques. What would he say when he saw her? She cheered herself by remembering how insistent he had been in his invitation to move to the chateau. She thought of his gallantry and his evident attraction to her and knew that the evening in Brussels had not been a dream.

She chanted under her breath, 'O my luve's like a red, red rose," then she sang louder, skipping along, brushing her hand lightly on the hawthorn branches arching over the lane so that showers of petals fell on her face and caught in her hair. Smiling to herself, Janine wondered how the thought of him could cause her mind, her heart, and her body to hold so much happiness.

She turned onto a wider road and crossed an ancient stone bridge spanning a stream. Just ahead, massive wrought-iron gates stood open amid a row of tall evergreens, which hid the chateau from view. As she stepped through the gate, she held her breath in disbelief.

Spread before her like a mirage, a medieval fortress complete with drawbridge appeared to float on the silvery waters of a lake. Surrounding the lake was a wide expanse of lawns and several sheep dotted the grass like giant puffballs. Janine was enchanted.

But now her problem was to find Jacques inside that pile

of bricks and stones. Would she dare to ring the doorbell? If she did, she would wake others besides him. She walked quietly over the gravel of the broad drive and stopped at the drawbridge. Jacques had said his window was surrounded by wisteria and looked out on a walled garden. If she could find it, she would throw a pebble into his room and wake him. She stifled a giggle. It seemed to her that the roles were reversed and Jacques should be the one under her window.

She crossed a rectangular cobblestoned courtyard, enclosed at one end by the rounded walls of squat towers, and walked through a Gothic archway opening into a walled garden. Looking up, scanning the facade of the castle, she saw a luxuriant vine draped with pale flowers; it climbed up the bricks of the east wing of the castle and surrounded a window whose gaping blackness was like a target encouraging her to try her aim.

Rooting around in a flower bed, she searched for a pebble, but all she could find was soft, crumbly dirt. She pressed the dirt into a little ball and threw it to Jacques's window, but the peatmoss disintegrated upon impact against a closed first-floor french window.

She began shaking the vine, but the only result was a shower of dew-laden petals and a whisper of trembling leaves. If Jacques was still awake, he'd think a breeze was ruffling the wisteria. She stared up at the window, jaws and fists clenched, focusing her will on him with the hope that her thoughts would draw him like a magnet. Unfortunately, it didn't work.

Discouraged, she grasped the woody part of the wisteria in her hands. The gnarled trunk was as thick as her thigh, and other parts of the vine twisted around it so that it wouldn't be difficult to find a hold for fingers and toes.

She removed her blazer and shoes, and grabbed a branch. With the scented blossoms tickling her exposed skin, she boosted herself up inch by inch. A moth brushed her lips. Wiping her mouth over her straining, outstretched arm, she whispered urgently, "Jacques!" She held her breath, waiting, hoping for his face to appear above.

The ground below was lost in shadows and from the lake a chorus of frogs mocked her. With her skirt swinging around her and a draft on her thighs, she forced herself to resume her climb.

When the windowsill was only a foot higher than the reach of her scrabbling fingers, she thought that with a final effort she could reach her goal, but just then the vine shuddered and there was a loud ripping sound. The branch she was holding on to dipped down, and she swung from it while her toes tried to find a foothold among the leaves. Was this the misfortune the owl had forecasted the previous night?

Her arms were weakening with the sustained effort and she inhaled deeply to find some strength just as a lightning bug flew under her nose and flickered its light. She clamped her mouth shut. If she had swallowed it, would she then always shine with an inner light?

"Jacques, help!" she screamed, and her voice echoed from the walls.

Even while worrying about her safety, she cringed at the thought of someone turning on floodlights and seeing her swinging twenty feet above the garden like Tarzan's mate. Perhaps the vine would drop her gently below into the garden.

"What in the world are you doing?" Jacques's voice was low and urgent and he looked like a light blur above her. He yanked back the vine and tried to reach her, but she had slipped and now was farther down.

"My early-morning calisthenics, what else?"

"Be quiet or you'll wake everybody up."

"Is lecturing during an emergency a compulsion of yours?" He had succeeded in pulling her against the wall once more and near its solidity she was feeling safer.

Leaning dangerously far out in his effort to reach her, he said, "If you don't lower your voice, this place will be a beehive of gossip by morning. Can you climb a tiny bit more?

I'll be able to reach you then and bring you inside. I must say I'm touched and overcome by your determination to be with me, but couldn't you have waited till morning?"

"I'm in no position to appreciate your humor. I'm slipping backward. The dew has made the branches slippery." She slid down two more inches and grabbed something in her teeth. A blossom broke off in her mouth and she spit it out. "Dammit, can't you do something? Are you afraid I'll take you down with me?" She remembered how she had yanked him into the pond and couldn't keep from smiling.

"Don't move. I'll be right back."

In a moment she felt a huge cloth smothering her and the light of the moon was blotted from view. What in the world was Jacques trying to do? She could hardly breathe with her face pressed by the heavy fabric into the delicately perfumed flowers of the vine.

"I'm holding on tight to the bedspread. Grab it and let me pull you up." His voice sounded muffled inside her wisteria-scented cocoon.

After repeated efforts, she finally was able to disengage her face and wrap her arms around the damask. As Jacques pulled, Janine felt herself being slowly lifted. As soon as her shoulders reached the windowsill, Jacques's strong fingers clasped her under the arms and pulled her inside. The tearing sound was from the hem of her skirt caught in the wisteria.

Trying to catch her breath, she plopped down on the floor and sat with her back against the wall, leaning her forehead against her bent knees.

He kneeled beside her and ruffled her hair with a tender, reassuring gesture. "This is the second time I've destroyed your clothes. I wonder if it's true that there are no accidents and that chance happenings are the ripples on the surface of life that show suppressed desires."

"If you look for deeper meanings, I'd hate to think of the symbolism you'd attach to my climb to reach your heights. It wasn't your fault my dress tore and I was foolish enough to do what I did." She inhaled deeply, trying to relieve her exhaustion.

"Yes, you were foolish. You could have been killed, and I can't even contemplate that possibility. I'd blame myself for the rest of my life. I telephoned you every fifteen minutes yesterday, and when no one answered I was terribly upset because I thought I'd scared you away and I'd never see you again."

His thumb caressed her temple and she shivered, not knowing whether it was from his touch or from the relief of her narrow escape. It seemed that since she had met Jacques her life had become entirely unmanageable.

"I kept thinking I'd find a hotel room in Brussels and then I'd ask you to meet me."

His kiss on her forehead was as light as a whisper. He began sniffing her skin and hair and his breath warmed her. "You smell like the incarnation of a wisteria blossom," he murmured with a catch in his voice. He placed one arm about her shoulders and said, "I'd like to think that you couldn't bear to wait any longer to see me, Janine, but I'm not that conceited. What happened?" Slipping the other arm under her knees, he lifted her.

"There was no room at the inn. I'll explain later," she said.

With her arms about his neck and her face nestled in the hollow of his throat, she inhaled the warm masculine scent of his skin. Gently he lowered her on his bed, which looked like a misty island in the dark sea of the invisible room, and she felt her head sink into the soft down pillows. She was so tired that she only wanted to drift into sleep.

Her eyelids flew open when she realized that Jacques was reclining next to her. He pulled her body to his and the heat of his skin made her tremble. "Oh, Jacques," she cried softly in a way that could have been either pleasure or despair.

Propped on one elbow, his eyes searched her face and his fingers traced her eyebrows as he murmured, "Say my name again, *chérie,* as you would call to your lover." His teeth nibbled the lobe of her ear and she felt a shudder travel down her neck, spine, and legs.

"Please, Jacques!" She couldn't tell what she was pleading for at that moment.

"I will please you, my darling. I'm overwhelmed at the thought that you spent the day searching for a hotel room for us, but, that was completely unnecessary. You should have let me make the arrangements."

"You are misunderstanding. I was only trying to find a place to live," she protested.

"Forgive me if I jumped to conclusions. I have thought of nothing else since I first glimpsed you. It's as if you had been created for me. But don't be afraid now, I won't rush you."

Her breath caught in her throat when he cupped her breast, and her nipples responded as his hand circled their hardness with a slow, deliberate motion. His mouth touched hers in a gentle kiss that at first was tentative, then became more demanding, and his arms clasped her to him and pressed her hard to the length of his body.

Stiffening in resistance, she tightened her lips, and when he sensed her withdrawal he held her more gently. Tenderly he kneaded her back and the tense muscles of her shoulders, and his lips changed from demanding to persuasive as he whispered, "Oh, Janine!"

With the tip of his tongue he began tracing her closed mouth. He nibbled at her lower lip and against her will she felt herself relaxing and accepting his probing.

The long kiss left them both breathless. His lips traveled over her cheeks and she closed her eyes. When he kissed her eyelids, she could feel her eyes pulsating under his touch like captured butterflies.

"You have the darkest and longest eyelashes I've ever seen. In the sun, their curve casts a shadow on your cheekbones and your eyes are framed by them like amethysts on black velvet." His fingers combed through her hair, then tugged one of her curls and let it spring back. His voice was husky and tender and soft when he murmured, "Your hair is as soft and silky as the wool of a newborn lamb."

She felt the passion in him and knew she would have to stop his searching hands, his questing lips, his seductive words, but her body was betraying her and her will seemed to melt with his caresses.

She whispered fiercely, "Look, I didn't come here for any hanky-panky!"

He stopped her mouth with a fierce kiss. Without releasing her, he lifted her over him and she felt the hardness of his body through his silk pajamas. Her heart hammered in her chest and her blood was on fire.

There was a hard edge to his voice when he said, "I already told you that's not my intention, and your choice of words doesn't suit my intentions. I'll make you my mistress, never doubt that for a second. When the time is right, I'll make love to you and you'll belong to me utterly. Now I'm only offering you an appetizer; you'll be asking for the rest of the banquet soon enough."

The words almost choked in her throat when she spluttered, "My choice of words might not sound right to you, but your own certainly sounds very quaint to me. I'll neither be your mistress nor your lover, Jacques, and I have no intention of becoming a notch on your gun."

He shook with silent laughter. "The symbolism of your metaphors would delight Freud, my dear."

With his hand at the nape of her neck, he pulled her face down and his mouth found hers again and in spite of herself she opened her lips to his probing, darting tongue. He pressed the other hand to the gentle swell of her hips and held her closer to him. She felt herself slide between his open knees and his strong thighs imprisoned her legs.

She raised her face and propped herself up on her elbows while his hips moved under hers. In the darkness of the room, his face was a pale blur and the dim light of the moon seemed to pinpoint lights of desire in his eyes. The sensations that had taken possession of her body were alarming, and she knew that if he insisted she wouldn't be able to resist him. Was this what she wanted? Her mind said *no*, but her body mocked her. Her heart was galloping like a runaway horse, and she was all too aware that all there was between her and Jacques was the flimsy material of their clothing, her weakening will, and his promise. But what kind of promise was it? He had only said, "when the time is right," and her primitive, raw responses might convince him that the time was now.

His hands were fumbling with the buttons of her blouse and she knew she should stop him, but her aching nipples craved the moistness of his mouth. He unfastened the front clasp of her lacy bra and her breasts spilled out. His mouth caressed her, and as she moaned deep in her throat, he took one nipple in his mouth, then moved to the other, and she pulled him closer to her breasts, pressing his face to her burning skin.

Without stopping what his tongue and lips were doing, his hand inched up her skirt and she felt the material moving up her legs with a silken rustling. His fingertips traveled along the velvet softness of her inner thigh and he murmured, "I've wanted to touch you here ever since I first saw you. Your skin is as delicate as a rose petal."

The sensations his caress elicited alarmed her. Was she ready to forget everything she had ever believed in and give herself to the sensuality that was engulfing her like a tidal wave? And why shouldn't he take what she had appeared to be offering? She was the one who had hurried through the night and climbed into his bedroom. He had only lifted her onto the bed. What else should he do but take the gift she was apparently offering? Every time her lips told him *no*, her body told him *yes* more clearly than her words of denial.

"Stop it, Jacques," she said, and pulled his hand away. "You said I'd be safe here, and just a moment ago you said, 'when the time is right.' I thought you meant right for me. We've just met and hardly know each other." She rolled off his body and buried her face into the pillow.

He stroked the nape of her neck. "You're like a scared doe,

chérie, and I'll not break my promise to you." His voice seemed to come from deep within him, as if she had awakened him from a dream. He sat up on the side of the bed and, leaning forward with his head between his hands, said, "The past twenty-four hours have dragged by as slowly as an entire month. I spent a terrible day worrying that I'd never see you again, and when you climbed into my room I felt as if I'd conjured you up."

When Janine gave him a censored version of her argument with Laure and told him how she had spent her day searching for a hotel room and forgotten her house key, he said, "It seems as if it was destined that you should accept my hospitality. I promise you'll be safe under my roof, just as if you were in a nunnery."

Reassured, she quipped, "I hope you don't mean a nunnery like the ones in Boccaccio's tales."

"I'm glad your sense of humor hasn't abandoned you, Will you stay?"

She snuggled her face against his chest and murmured, "Yes. There's nothing I'd like better, Jacques, if you'll back off and stop pressing me."

"You have my word that I won't ever force you into anything you don't want to do." His tone was light and self-assured.

He got up and smiled down at her. Picking up his robe from the back of a chair, he slipped it on and walked to the window, where he stared down into the courtyard. "The leaves on the flagstones below look as if a Kansas tornado had crossed the Atlantic and homed in on the wisteria. I feel as if I've been caught in a whirlwind myself," he said.

She felt exactly the same way. Sitting up on the side of the bed, she looked at the ripped hem of her skirt. Feeling dizzy, she wiggled her bare toes in the thick carpet and said, "I left my shoes and jacket below."

He leaned out the window. "I don't see them. I guess I'd better go find them and take you to a guest room before the servants wake up."

Feeling dazed, she stood up, and in walking to the

window tripped against a small round table. Trying to regain her balance, she knocked over a massive brass lamp, which rolled on the Persian carpet and clattered onto the parquet floor. Janine covered her mouth with her hand. Two seconds later there was a knock on the door.

Four

The door opened a crack and a blond girl wearing hexagonal glasses peered in and whispered, "Are you all right, Jacques?"

Jacques rushed to the door. "Of course I am. Go back to bed, Monette," he replied as he tried to ease her out of the room.

Slipping under his arm, Monette closed the door behind her and leaned against it. "In a minute. It's such a relief to find out it's only a girl. A while ago I thought a leopard had escaped from the zoo and was slithering up the vine." With an intrigued smile on her pixie face, she advanced on Janine and offered her hand. "I'm Monette de Turenne, and you don't know how happy I am to see that Jacques has a girlfriend. That sort of takes the responsibility off my hands."

Embarrassed at being discovered in Jacques's room and puzzled by the newcomer's last statement, Janine shook her hand and introduced herself, while Jacques stepped to her side and encircled her shoulder with a protective gesture.

Monette plopped on the bed and studied the couple with a mischievous, interested look. Her straight shoulder-length hair bobbed with her motion like the silk fringe of a shawl, and her smocked white cotton nightgown enhanced her childlike appearance.

Jacques's frustration at the invasion of his privacy was evident from the way he tightened his jaws as he said, "You must have been having quite a dream, Monette, and you're still not quite awake. I have to go downstairs now and get her shoes and jacket. I'll be back in a minute." Then he whispered to Janine, "Don't worry about her. She's an oddball, but really quite harmless."

Left alone, the two girls smiled at each other. Monette's look was so friendly that Janine nearly overcame her discomfort. Leaning against the windowsill, she said, "I'm really not his girl friend. We only just met. Sometimes a situation gives the wrong impression."

"Don't worry. I make no moral judgments."

Janine decided it would be better to drop the subject, because the more she protested, the worse it would sound. Remembering Monette's puzzling statement, she asked, "What did you mean saying you were relieved of the responsibility? What responsibility?"

"Of having to tell my parents I wouldn't like Jacques for a husband. Now I can say he's interested in somebody else."

"But I'll only be here a little while and that excuse won't hold up very long." She swallowed and, afraid of the answer, asked, "Are you engaged to him?" The thought of Jacques making love to Monette made her tremble with anguish and yet she couldn't bring herself to dislike this girl.

"Oh, no! He's one of many I've been paraded before and supposed to entice. I'm like the sauce that's meant to make the entrée more appetizing."

"The entrée?"

"That's my dowry. For two summers my parents have been sending me to the homes of relatives and friends where there are eligible males. They want to marry me off, but I won't cooperate. If you ever hear me whinny it's because I'm starting to feel like a prize filly they're trying to mate to a thoroughbred stallion, and I don't like it. But I'm running out of excuses. What fault could I ever find with Jacques? He's perfect."

"Isn't the fact that you don't love him reason enough?"

"They tell me I could learn to, and I daresay he's charming and very sexy, but the reason I wouldn't marry him or anybody else is that I'm already in love."

"Do they know?" Janine asked, and wondered how Jacques felt about Monette.

"Yes, but they think Francois Beaumont is unsuitable. What do you think of him?"

"Francois Beaumont? I don't believe I know him."

"He knows you. He met you at the Café Central the other night. He's a veterinarian and just graduated in June. You can't have forgotten him. He's twenty-three, has brown hair, and wears hornrimmed glasses." From the way Monette's face lighted up as she continued describing Francois, Janine could tell how much in love she was, and a picture of the young man began to form in her memory. He had been attractive and friendly, but unimpressive, and she had barely noticed him in the bustle of the café.

"Yes, I believe I remember him. He seems very nice. Why is he unsuitable?" Unbidden came the thought that if a veterinarian would not be a suitable match for Monette, a schoolteacher would be no better for Jacques.

"It's the same old story in this decadent society. People aren't judged by their merits but by their family connections and their wealth. His mother's a widow and is in trade. She owns a little bakery in Lillois and she's a real darling. Unfortunately, Francois doesn't have a job yet, but he's trying."

Monette jumped off the bed and came very close to Janine. She lowered her voice, but her tone had absolute determination when she said, "When I reach my twenty-first birthday, I mean to elope with Francois. Hopefully by that time he'll be financially independent and we won't need anybody's help. It's certain I won't see a penny of my dowry."

Just then Jacques returned with the shoes and blazer

and handed them to Janine together with a pair of his pajamas. Shooing Monette out of his room, he led Janine down a long corridor lighted only dimly by the dawn lighting a lead-glass window at the far end.

The guest room's heavy draperies were drawn and Jacques turned on a tall bronze lamp that cast a subdued light on the pale Chinese carpet, the graceful Empire furniture, and the blue-canopied bed recessed in an alcove. The shape of the bed with its curved foot- and headboards made Janine think of Cleopatra's barge. Her Antony, wearing a robe and silk pajamas instead of a Roman toga, stood before the open door.

"I'll tell the butler not to let the servants wake you up. Sleep as late as you want." He took a step backward, as if eager to leave.

Feeling the ripped hem of her skirt dangling against her leg, she said, "I need to get my suitcases and I also should let Uncle Pierre know where I'm staying."

"Don't worry about anything. I'll stop at the café and have a talk with your uncle. When you wake up you'll find your belongings outside your room." He leaned against the doorjamb, surveying her, and she felt as if his gaze were drawing her to him like a magnet.

Filled with the power of his presence and her own desire to touch him, she looked up at him and opened her lips. His broad shoulders, his tousled hair falling across his forehead, and the mat of blond hair revealed by the open neck of his pajamas made her want to run her hands across his chest and to feel his mouth against her own.

He pulled her to him for an instant, then with his thumb on her chin he lowered her head. Kissing her forehead, he murmured, "Oh no you don't! My willpower has limits and they've been stretched to the breaking point tonight. Give me time to recuperate." He turned her around and, giving her a gentle push, ordered, "Go to sleep now. I'll see you in a few hours." There was an amused tone in his voice, and looking over her shoulder, she saw his lips quirk in the crooked grin that she found so appealing.

She went to sit on the bed and said, "All right, Jacques. You're not upset with me, are you?"

"Of course not. I had promised that you'd be safe here, but when I felt you responding to me, my mind disconnected from my body. I wanted you absolutely. I should be the one to apologize, but I won't. I'd feel like a hypocrite."

Janine stared at her lap and nodded. "I know what you mean, Jacques."

"Even talking about it is weakening my resolve. If you held your arms out to me right now, I'd dive into your bed and tear your clothes off," he teased, still lounging against the door, but his body looked tense and ready to spring.

She cleared her throat and held his gaze. "If we want a chance to know each other better, we'll have to keep cool, I guess."

He laughed. "I'm anything but that. Too bad that you don't attach the biblical meaning to the verb *know.* Good night now," he said. He stepped into the hall and closed the door behind him.

For a long moment she stared at the spot where he had stood, then she undressed and snuggled in the bed. Within seconds she was asleep.

When she woke, at first she couldn't remember where she was, then the silkiness of the pajamas Jacques had lent her caressed her skin and reminded her of his warm, hard body pressed to hers. She stretched under the blue satin sheets and the memories flooded back with such incredible force that every part of her body tingled and seemed to beg for his touch.

Sighing, she jumped out of bed and opened the blue velvet drapes and the casement window. The morning was cool and pleasant and the scent of flowers drifted from the formal gardens on the soft breeze. Twenty feet below, the lake surrounding the castle shimmered in the sun. In the distance was a white building that looked like a summer pavilion or a garden house supported by columns.

Her suitcases were outside her door, and the crystal bud vase with the red rose perched on her portable typewriter spoke to her of the romantic evening in Brussels. So many things had happened since and the relationship had heated up so quickly that the innocent evening seemed to have taken place weeks before. She placed the vase on the desk before the window and the flaming petals of the full-blown rose seemed to underscore the fire and ripeness of her feelings.

After she unpacked and showered, she dressed in a pair of designer jeans and a red-and-white-checked blouse. Looking at herself in the mirror framed against the luxurious background, she thought that her western togs looked incongruous in these surroundings. As she brushed her hair, she wondered if she had done the right thing in letting Jacques face Pierre. Her uncle was her only living blood relative, and she would have to call him or stop at the café to show him she didn't hold him responsible for what had happened, even though the thought of seeing Laure again was disagreeable.

A piping sound, muffled by her closed door, interrupted her reverie. Listening more closely, she realized the tune sounded strangely like the "Star-Spangled Banner," but the rendition was different and the tempo was a trifle slower than usual. Opening her door, she followed the sound of pure, clear notes and found herself in Monette's bedroom.

Dressed in a red ankle-length gypsy skirt and sleeveless gold-lamé blouse in the style of the twenties, Monette was leaning over a large mahogany table where dozens of brandy snifters partially filled with water lined the table. With the graceful movements of a ballerina, the girl's damp fingertips rubbed around the glass rims and played the American national anthem.

On seeing Janine, she paused and said, "I thought maybe that would bring you out, even though I know the tempo isn't quite right yet. Have you had breakfast?"

"No. Have you?"

"I thought I'd wait for you. I'll order brioches, orange

juice, and coffee, unless you'd prefer a full American breakfast."

Janine opted for the brioches, and while Monette called the kitchen on the telephone intercom, she wondered where Jacques was.

During the few minutes they waited for their meal, Monette gave a rendition of "Home on the Range" in honor of Janine's western attire.

"You play quite well," Janine remarked when the song ended.

"I practice a lot. I enjoy this more than playing the piano or the violin. Did you know that in 1791 Mozart composed a piece for unaccompanied brandy snifters?" Monette proceeded to play it while Edith, a young maid in a black uniform, served breakfast and lingered in the doorway to listen.

Sitting on dainty chairs covered in mauve velvet drawn up to a small table, they ate and chatted and Monette said, "I wish I could raise some money and cut a record. With the right promotion I could sell it."

"Are you after money or fame?" Janine asked as she sipped her coffee.

"Since my parents found out about Francois, they keep me broke all the time. That's how they try to control me. I used to have quite a large allowance, but lately I only have a credit card for gasoline and a pittance that's hardly enough for walking-around money." She went back to the brandy snifters and began playing the "Song of the Volga Boatmen," and while the somber notes filled the room and drifted into the walled garden, she said, "I have an idea of how I could get some cash, but I'll need your help."

Janine asked hesitantly, "What do you want me to do?"

"There's a village fair in Orpe Le Petit tomorrow. Don't you think I could raise some money by giving an open-air concert there?"

"Will they let you?"

"Sure. Anybody can set up a booth or a display. All I need

is for you to pass the hat and collect the coins. Of course a monkey with a tin cup would attract more attention."

She chewed her knuckle and studied Janine, who laughed and replied, "Even wearing a costume, I'd be too tall to look like a chimp. To tell you the truth, passing the hat doesn't appeal to me at all, with or without a costume. I have seen street musicians collect donations in an open guitar case set on the ground. People just throw coins in. I'd be willing to help you set up and give you moral support during the performance."

"I'll need a large table, but it wouldn't fit in my car. Also, we'll have to carry jugs of water so I could fill the glasses after I set up." Monette's pixie face was flushed with excitement.

"I'll call my uncle and ask him if we can borrow a table. We can also get the water in the café so we won't have to tote full jugs."

"That's great. Call him right now." Monette twirled about the room, showing an expanse of flounced petticoats and a pair of coltish legs.

Janine dialed the number of the Café Central. Even though she knew that she didn't need to make any excuses and that her relatives would have to accept her decision to spend a few days at the chateau, her heart hammered in her chest and her hands were ice cold. Dreading that her aunt would answer, she felt relieved when she heard Pierre's voice.

"Uncle Pierre, this is Janine. I didn't want you to worry about me. I am at the Laurents', and Monette de Turren is here too and we're having fun together." Her words tumbled out quickly, as if she didn't want to give Pierre a chance to comment or cajole.

"I know, child. Monsieur Laurent was here earlier this morning. But don't you think you should come home? Laure is terrible sorry about the things she said and . . ."

Janine heard the extension being picked up in the back room of the café. "Janine, my dear, will you ever forgive me?" Laure pleaded. "If you'll just come home, I promise I won't criticize anything you do, either by word or look. Please say you've forgiven me."

With a sigh Janine replied, "Yes, Aunt Laure, I forgive you. Let's not talk about it anymore now so we can both forget what happened." Laure's words still rankled and she hoped that soon their memory would fade.

"Will you come back, then? Think of your reputation and our good name, if for no other reason."

There it was again, Janine thought, shaking her head. "No, I won't, but I'll visit."

She heard a sniffle at the other end, then Pierre came back on the line. "Do whatever you think best, Janine, and don't forget that you'll always be welcome at our home."

"Thanks," she said, feeling better for having called. Just then she heard a plaintive note and turned to see Monette pointing frantically to the brandy snifters. Remembering her promise, she asked Pierre if they could borrow a table the following day. Pierre consented without hesitation and they said goodbye on a fairly cheerful note.

Too restless to sit still, Janine decided to arrange an interview with Monsieur Fronville. When she called Jacques's partner, he immediately consented to see her as soon as she could get to his house.

Just as Janine was saying, "Would you also let me take some photographs of you, Monsieur Fronville?" Jacques entered the room and stepped to her side.

His presence seemed to fill the room. Looking at his well-muscled shoulders and the sunlight streaking highlights in his blond hair, Janine knew she had been wanting to see him ever since she had opened her eyes. Her smile turned into a frown when Jacques took the telephone away from her before she could hear Fronville's answer.

The joy of seeing him was erased by a surge of anger and she clenched her fists and stared at him, her eyes burning with fire. Jacques was treating her like a child. When he had invited her to be his guest, he had said she could come and go as she pleased, and now he was breaking his promise.

"Philippe, I'm sorry, but the appointment'll have to be canceled. Mademoiselle Heerlen didn't know I had made plans for us. We're going riding and our horses are already saddled." He listened for a moment, then replied, "That's not it at all. You'll have a chance to meet her at the dance. There's no point in her interviewing you. You haven't been to the United States, and what's more, you know nothing about American wines. Whatever you'd tell her would be inaccurate." His laughter at Fronville's response had a sarcastic undertone, then he abruptly said goodbye.

"I didn't appreciate that at all," Janine said, and bit her lip to control its trembling. What she really wanted to do was pick up the telephone and hit Jacques over the head with it.

"I can tell, but what you heard is the truth. All he did was put up a small amount of cash. If you're so determined to write a feature on the subject, I'll give you the facts myself."

Ignoring their argument, Monette moved her arms over the mahogany table and caressed the glass rims, bringing forth notes of "La Marseillaise" while the sun, slanting through the window, refracted rainbows of light through the crystal and onto the ivory damask walls.

Janine was still upset, but she knew she would rather get the information she wanted from Jacques than from a man she had never met. Changing the subject, but still resenting his behavior, she said, "What dance are you talking about? I never said I'd go."

"You won't have to go anywhere. It'll be here at the chateau in a few days and you can sit in your room and pout if you think that'll give you more pleasure." He took her arm and propelled her out of the room.

"I'll see you at lunch, Monette," Janine called over her shoulder.

"No, you won't. I'm eating in my room. I have to practice some new songs," Monette called after her.

Janine turned to Jacques as they descended the stairs to the walled garden and said, "How do you know I'll still be here?"

"I know." He pulled her to him and kissed her full on the mouth. Then, as if nothing had happened, he continued, "Stop being so touchy. You wanted an interview and I'm submitting. What else do you need to make you happy?" He draped his arm around her shoulders and squeezed her to him. Bending toward her, he whispered in her ear, "I'll give you anything you want, and more."

She felt goosebumps rising on her arms and back. Scowling, she stopped in the walled garden they had just entered. Pulling away from him, she said, "Don't do what you just did ever again. You could have told me and I could have called Fronville back and canceled the appointment myself."

"You're right and I apologize, but there's something else you don't know. Philippe's an old libertine and I'll not allow you to be alone with him."

"Come on, Jacques! Give me credit for knowing how to handle myself."

He cleared his throat, but his voice had a rough edge when he said, "He's all charm and he might try to take you away from me."

"Jacques, I don't belong to you," she said as an elderly gardener tipped his cap as they passed. The pile of leaves at his feet spoke of the previous night's climb and she wondered if everyone in the chateau knew of her escapade.

They walked through the gothic archway and traversed the rectangular cobblestoned courtyard. With a self-assured smile Jacques said, "It's true you don't belong to me . . . yet, but I'll not allow any poachers in my territory."

Janine snapped, "You make me sound like a game preserve. Or would *fair game* be the appropriate word?"

There was a steel edge in his voice when he replied, "Don't underestimate me. You'll be mine, and if Philippe or anyone else tries anything with you, they'll live to regret it."

They were crossing the drawbridge as she said, "Till you tire of the game and feel there's no more challenge, right?"

He grasped her arm and yanked her to him. "This is no game and I'll never tire of you."

She shook herself free and rubbed the imprints his fingers had made on her skin. "Of course not. There won't be time. I'll conveniently leave before that happens."

"Janine, I know you're still angry about the telephone. Please, let's forget the incident and enjoy each other's company. I'm sorry if I was rough. You really provoked me and I didn't realize I squeezed your arm so hard. I can't bear for you to talk about us that way." His eyes held pride and concern as he gazed down at her and she felt ashamed of her remarks.

She nodded as they walked toward the groom who was trying to control Jacques's stallion. Max was pawing the ground and sniffing the nostrils of a fine sorrel mare. The mare whinnied softly and nuzzled the stallion's neck.

Jacques and Janine mounted their horses and cantered side-by-side through the wrought-iron gates. He sat his horse with relaxed style; and Janine, forgetting their argument and his possessiveness, let the pleasure of riding at his side flood her consciousness.

The white pines bordering the Laurents' estate gave way to a row of chestnut trees. On the opposite side of the road, blue spruce screened what appeared to be another estate. Janine smiled at a red-haired boy who was swinging to and fro on a gate among the spruce trees.

"*Merci* for opening up, Antoine," Jacques called to the child and threw him a coin.

Antoine caught it with a leap and his grin disclosed a gap where he had lost his baby teeth. As soon as they rode through, he latched the gate behind them.

Of common accord, Jacques and Janine began galloping, Jacques slightly ahead to show the way. The horses jumped across a small stream and over a low wall, then galloped over fields of clover and alfalfa till they came upon a manor house with boarded-up windows and four tall chimneys sprouting from a tangle of brambles and ivy. Suddenly Jacques pulled up short and the stallion reared. Janine's heart raced in fear for him, but in a moment Jacques had his mount under control and was leaning across his neck to pet and soothe him. Janine admired his skill.

"You had me worried for a minute," she said, realizing how inadequate her words were. The thought of him lying injured at her feet had sent a wave of terror through her and her knees were still trembling.

"It's all right. It was really my fault. I shouldn't have pulled him up so short." He pointed to the manor house. "Do you know where you are?"

Janine looked at the abandoned place, at several out-buildings with broken windows, at an open stable now used to store farm machinery, and at the wide expanse of land. Suddenly she knew. "Yes. It's Les Alouettes," she murmured.

Looking at the creepers that nearly covered the pale brick walls, at the purple clematis and white bellflowers that perhaps her own grandmother had planted, at the trees her father and uncle might have climbed as children, at the very ground upon which her forebears had trod for centuries, Janine felt a knot in her throat. This was her ancestral home.

They resumed the ride at a leisurely pace and soon a thicket of cedars hid Les Alouettes from view.

Jacques's voice was tender when he said, "You might have been born and reared here instead of so far away."

"I'm here now." She realized that her unspoken statement was, *It's up to you to keep me.*

"I'll well aware of that." His tone was bantering, but his gray eyes bored through her and her blood rushed hotly through her veins.

As they entered a narrow lane where they had to ride single file, she replied, "Of course, it wouldn't have been me. I would have had a different mother."

"Then sometimes things happen for the best, wouldn't you agree? But look there now."

On the left of the track, an old, whitewashed, conical building covered on one side by Virginia creeper dominated an elm thicket. Pink bricks showed through the deteriorating walls. The mill was crowned by an overhanging slate roof, and Janine thought that it must have been abandoned long ago.

"How quaint," she said, reining in her horse in the brick-paved courtyard. Grass and chickweed grew between the bricks.

They dismounted and hitched their horses to ancient rings on the mill's wall. Then Janine followed Jacques to a door covered with peeling green paint. Jacques removed a brick near the stone lintel and extracted an old iron key from the recess.

"Come on, we'll walk to the top and look at the view," he said.

The door squeaked on rusty hinges and Jacques closed it behind them. Beams of light streaming through the deeply recessed windows seemed to converge on a mammoth millstone in the center of the building. The rust on shafts, chains, and pulleys confirmed the machinery's long disuse.

Jacques preceded her up a creaking, corkscrew stairway and all the way up she watched his long, muscular legs and his narrow hips molded by his riding britches. The male power emanating from his body was a palpable presence in the deserted mill. When they reached a round room at the top, through paneless windows they saw the chateau mirrored on its lake; Les Alouettes, forlorn and abandoned; Nivelle with its ancient cathedral; the pyramid at Waterloo; a train chugging over a distant trestle; farmhouses like forts surrounding their inner courtyards; and a checkerboard of fields, ponds, and streams. Swallows crisscrossed the china blue sky.

Jacques snapped his handkerchief over a rustic bench and, inviting Janine to sit down, said, "I'll give you the interview now, if you wish."

Sitting on the bench with her, he told her that on his lands he raised hops, wheat, sugar beets, and prize Charolais cattle. The corner of his mouth turned up in a half-smile when he began talking about the vineyards his family had owned along the river Meuse. He said, "But, because of French competition, the vineyards became unprofitable in the twenties, long before I was born. The vines were plowed under and the land was put to more gainful use. We've been raising excellent hothouse grapes, but it's a limited crop. We use all of it to make sparkling wine for our private use. Five years from now, though, when the new grapevines I planted in Missouri begin to bear fruit, there'll be Chateau Laurent wines again." He moved closer to her and his arm brushed hers.

She inched away. With her pen poised on an old envelope Jacques had given her to write on, she said, "That's what I really want to learn about. I didn't know wine grapes could be grown in the Midwest. I thought New York and California were the only states with a suitable climate."

Jacques looped his arm around her waist and drew her back against him. "Do you really want to spend the morning talking about viticulture?" He raised her chin, and his eyes were the color of charcoal.

She jumped up and the pen clattered to the floor. "Look, it was evident when I first asked you in Brussels that you didn't want to be bothered with this, yet you embarrassed me and made me look foolish when I tried another source. I can neither concentrate nor take notes when you hold me close, and at present my only wish is to communicate on an intellectual level!"

He stood before her and, wrapping his arms about her, pulled her to him. "I know, *chérie*, but what happens when I'm near you is that my sexuality, my emotions, and my intellect become one and I can't keep my hands off you."

He kissed her full on the mouth and she tried to push him away, but his words also applied to what she was feeling, and in a second she felt herself melting into his embrace. Her arms looped around his neck while her body responded to his hot, pressing reality.

His mouth traveled along her cheek to her neck and ear and she shuddered with the pleasurable sensations that coursed along every inch of her body. "Your lips taste like Villard Blanc grapes warmed by the sun and your skin has the bouquet of the Leon Millots that produce such delicious Burgundy wines." His tongue traced her delicate ear and he whispered, "Those are the vinifera grapes in my Missouri acreage."

She laughed. "Jacques, I'm not a vineyard."

"But you're almost ready for the harvest," he replied, unbuttoning her shirt. He buried his face in her bosom, and his voice was husky and tender when he said, "I'm doing my best to give you the details you need, but right now I want to drink of the fruit of the vine." He unfastened the front clasp of her bra and his tongue circled her erect nipple, then his mouth fastened on it and she threw back her head, giving herself up to the pleasure of the instant.

When he raised his head, his eyes were glazed and he cupped her hips and pulled her against him. "Touch me, Janine. I want to feel your hands on my body."

Reaching for the buttons of his shirt, she began undoing them one by one, till his chest, covered by thick blond hair, stood revealed. She buried her face in it and kissed him, softly and lingeringly. Reaching inside his open shirt, she slipped her arms around his back and clasped him tightly. The hard muscles of his back tightened under her touch and their bare torsos strained against each other.

Jacques threw his shirt to the floor, then slid her bra and blouse off her shoulders and let them fall at her feet. He devoured her with his eyes, and she stood still and straight, proud of her femininity, which responded to his maleness with primitive instincts she had not known she possessed.

He clasped her to him and their bare skin seemed to catch fire as they wrapped each other more tightly in their embrace. "You feel so right in my arms and I have wanted to see your beauty revealed ever since I heard your voice from the shadows of the willow tree," he whispered in her ear. His fingers trembled as he began fumbling with the belt of her jeans.

She grasped his hands and pulled them away. "Jacques, I can't bear this much longer. You set me on fire every time you touch me and I feel as if soon I'll have no strength left to deny you."

"Or yourself?"

"Or myself." She scooped up her clothes and dressed, her back to him.

Coming up behind her, he nuzzled her neck. "Will you let me see you undressed if I give you my word I'll not take you against your will?"

"My will doesn't deserve its name anymore. A moment ago I wanted to lie down on the bare boards and pull you on top of me."

"I know. I read it in your eyes. But I'd never take you here. I want to make love to you for hours, on a soft bed where my weight won't crush you, my darling."

"I wanted to be crushed and melt into you." She walked to a window so he wouldn't see the flush that was slowly spreading on her face. Far away, a slow-moving barge looked like a gray snail gliding on grass. Closer at hand she saw a brilliant light as if the sun were reflecting on a mirror. At the edge of the brilliance she could barely distinguish the weeping willow. That was their pond, she thought.

He stood behind her at the window and she felt his breath in her hair. "Let's go to the pond, Janine." His voice cracked with desire.

"I feel too vulnerable right now. We'd better go back to the chateau."

"I won't make love to you. There is no time. My step-mother is expecting us for lunch. I only want to look at you and touch you. If I had wanted to take you, I'd have come into your bed last night, and I don't believe you'd have sent me away. Will you come?"

She remembered the clear water, the white sand, the shade of the willow tree, and the yellow weeds and butter-cups that had seemed to invite her to stretch at his side. Did she trust herself to return there with Jacques? "Promise?" she whispered, knowing by his urgent fingers kneading her waist that he would promise anything and that it would be up to her once again to put on the brakes.

"Yes! Yes!" He pulled her by the hand and they hurried down the stairway.

Five

When they reached the pond, he tethered the horses in the shade of an elder. Jacques and Janine stood facing each other on the grassy bank. The perfume of honeysuckle and wild mint enveloped the glade. Listening to the song of a lark, Janine felt as if the god Pan were playing his seductive reed pipes in their honor.

Hugging her arms, Janine stared down at a blue butterfly on a white daisy nestled in the grass. Her heart was fluttering like its wings and she felt as if she had been transported to another age and was about to perform some pagan rite. Had she really consented to let Jacques see her unclothed? She lowered her head farther and wondered at her own desire to look at him and feel his bare skin against the entire length of her body.

Jacques lifted her chin and looked into her eyes. "Don't be afraid, darling. We'll have to leave in half an hour." As he talked his husky voice seemed to weave a spell in the sunny glade and his fingers were slow and gentle as he unfastened her blouse, her belt buckle, and the clasp of her bra. He dropped her clothes to the ground and knelt before her, burying his face in her soft abdomen. His lips traced a path around her navel and lower while his hands held the curve of her hips against his questing mouth. She shivered under the relentless velvet of his touch, and the pleasure that engulfed her when his tongue traced the satiny skin of her inner thigh made her gasp. She knew she was weakening and her femininity was prodding her to capitulate to his seductive, practiced mouth. She moaned as she dug her fingernails into the hard muscles of his shoulders.

His smile was knowing when he stood up. "I told you there's no time," he said, removing his clothes with quick, hurried gestures.

Her eyes took in his incredibly handsome physique, all taut muscles, sinews, and golden hairs. It was as if the statue of a Greek god had come to life in the enchanted glade.

Taking her hand, he pulled her into the pond and she swam away from him, cooling her burning skin, her entire consciousness filled with the powerful look of his body. He was the first man she had ever seen naked and she knew the sight would stay with her for the rest of her life.

The strength of his desire for her needed no words on his part. His eyes and his touch asserted his need to possess her completely, and she knew that if their positions were reversed, no protest or promise would stand in the way of their physical union.

He caught up with her and they treaded water while his hand caressed her face. "Thank you, Janine. I wanted to look at you here at the pond and you've given me a gift I'll treasure forever."

Moving closer to him, she pressed herself against him and their slick, wet bodies added another dimension to the pleasure of their contact. "We can't keep this up, you know. It's too difficult for me," she whispered.

"You can choose to go with your feelings. You'd be surprised how delightful it'll be if you'll only stop processing everything through your brain. You have as much right to follow the dictates of your body as those of your mind, and I guarantee that the rewards will meet with your approval. You'll wonder what made us waste so much time in all these preliminaries."

He grasped her just above the knees and wrapped her legs

about his hips. Open to him in the buoyancy of the water, her own lips searched for his while she clasped him about the neck. His tongue plunged into the silkiness of her damp mouth while his powerful maleness caressed the center of her feminine desire.

"Oh, Jacques," she moaned, moving against him while his hands on her buttocks guided her gently.

She closed her eyes and completely abandoned herself to her feelings, which seemed to be lifting her up and up to she knew not where. She opened them when he unwrapped her legs from his hips.

"Come," he said as he pulled her back to the shore.

She stood dazed on the grassy bank and watched him grab their clothes and spread them in the tall yellow weeds to create a hidden nest for them.

He picked her up and lowered her in the bower he had fashioned while their hearts hammered against each other.

Covering her eyes with her arm, she trembled and moaned while he kissed her lips. Then his mouth traveled to her breasts and down the length of her body, slowly and lingeringly. Her hips arched to his mouth and suddenly fireworks of sensations lifted her into another sphere of being, where she neither heard nor saw but was in a kaleidoscope of pleasure. Her only reality was her own body, awakened and throbbing.

With the release of her pent-up desires, she sobbed his name. "Oh, Jacques!"

He kissed her tenderly on the lips and whispered against her mouth, *"Chérie,"* while his fingers pushed back the damp tendrils of hair from her forehead and traced soft patterns on her breasts and stomach.

In a few moments she forced herself to sit up. Feeling emptied and weak, she clasped her arms about her knees to hide her nakedness.

Gazing into the burning gray eyes of this man who had taken her to a dream world and revealed her own body to her, she wondered how she could ever bear to give him up.

Lying at her side, he traced her shoulder blades and then

her spine with a finger. "Jacques, I don't want an affair, and there's no time for a relationship." She felt selfish and embarrassed at her own statement. He had given pleasure and she had taken it without offering anything in return.

"Time is an illusion. We could live a lifetime in a week."

"And I'd be left with a memory and the longing to be with you."

"But that would be a choice you'd make. You can stay with me."

"I have to return home." The word sounded nonsensical. Her home was in his arms.

"Not if you don't want to," he insisted.

"But I have a contract. If I break it, my teaching career will be at an end before it begins. I'd lose my certificate!"

"Trust me, darling. I can arrange everything and get you out of the contract. I could refurbish Les Alouettes, and I'd see you almost every day, for as long as we want." He sat up and his arms went around her waist. Resting his chin on her shoulder and nuzzling her neck, he said, "Don't keep denying us."

"Enough, Jacques. Please don't talk about it anymore."

"I can't understand your stubbornness. You'll not consent to an affair because you want a relationship. When I offer that, you find other difficulties. What do you want? And don't tell me you don't want me, because I know better."

She stood up and put on her clothes over her sun-warmed body.

"If you're determined to teach, I can use my influence and find you a post at the American school that is attended by the children of NATO personnel," he said, buttoning his shirt.

"Or you could move to Kansas City," she said. The idea of being stashed away at Les Alouettes was preposterous, and why should she give up her country and her career and be his mistress or, more accurately, his kept woman? She seriously doubted that he could actually find her a position in Brussels.

He laughed and said, "But, Janine, I have responsibilities here. My father is in his seventies and can't look after the estate any longer even with the help of our agent. I can't leave my home. My family has lived here for centuries."

"Yet you want me to abandon my country, my home, and my friends, till you get tired of our liaison, and then it'll be up to me to pick up the pieces."

"You underestimate yourself, my dear. Couldn't it be possible that you're projecting on me what you think you'll do? I can't foresee ever getting tired of you."

"Let's stop this conversation, please," she said as he pulled her close to him and kissed her eyes and her cheeks. Before he could reach her mouth, she pushed him away and with a trembling voice said, "I don't want us to do this anymore. Let's try to just be friends, and when and if you come to Kansas City, you can call me, if you want to."

He released her and his laughter echoed in the glade. Shaking his head, he said, "Come on, it's time to go. Keep the illusion we can be just friends, if you want to have childish fantasies. My own fantasies are of a completely different type. The only thing is, mine will come true and yours won't because you won't let them and neither will I."

They remounted their horses and trotted down the lane to the chateau, leaving the enchanted pond and the perfume of honeysuckle behind.

"You love Kansas City, don't you?" he asked. His face didn't reveal his feelings, and it was as if they were only acquaintances enjoying a country ride. "I like the wide boulevards, the clean air, the attractive buildings, but, of course, most of all the friendly people." He grinned at her and his leg brushed hers.

"Of course I love it. It's my hometown." The horses had slowed to a walk and the sound of a tractor in a distant field brought with it the scent of new-mown hay. At its zenith, the sun heated Janine's back and she felt her long-sleeved shirt sticking to her back.

"It's not much compared to New York or Chicago, but it has its charm," he agreed.

Nearing the castle, the horses began to trot and Jacques loosened the reins and gave Max his head. Janine caught up to him as they rode into the courtyard.

They dismounted and handed the reins to the groom, who had come to meet them. Martin led the horses toward the stables while the child, Antoine, played with a little mound of rocks and grinned at them with his gapped smile. Looking down at the child, Janine thought how much had happened to her since she had first seen him at the beginning of the morning ride. It seemed to her that she had discovered an entire new dimension.

"My stepmother is expecting us. When the weather permits, she lunches in the garden house. You'll enjoy it," Jacques said, removing some grass from her hair.

She followed him along the gravelled path leading to the round building nestled like a forest temple among the ancient oaks. The chateau was reflected on the clear lake on their right, and the spicy odor of geraniums vied with the subtle scent of roses in the formal gardens, visible through openings in the tall boxwood hedge.

At the end of the path, Janine and Jacques mounted the three white-stone steps that circled the round building. The garden pavilion was open on all sides, and the narrow masonry walls sandwiched between pillars at the four points of the compass created the illusion of a colonnade supporting the mansard roof.

The shelter was furnished in wicker and rattan with bold-print cushions on chaises and chairs. Seated by one of the windows, Madame Francine Laurent, in an aqua linen sheath, sipped an aperitif and smoked a gold-tipped cigarette. The table, set for three, was covered by a blue tablecloth hand-embroidered with white tulips, and the crystal and silver sparkled in a shaft of sunlight.

"*Bon jour*, madame," Jacques said, bending toward her without touching his lips to the proffered hand.

"*Bon jour*, Jacques," she replied in a throaty voice. "I was beginning to wonder if you had forgotten." Her coquettish smile accentuated the deep lines that ran between her nose and her thin lips. She plumped the waves of her graying hair softly twisted into a chignon at the nape of her neck.

"The day was so beautiful for horseback riding that Mademoiselle Heerlen and I almost lost track of the time."

For the first time Madame Laurent let her gaze drift to Janine, who had stood back waiting. The older woman smiled, but the smile did not warm her hazel eyes, and Janine had the distinct impression that Madame Laurent found her Western outfit gaudy and ridiculous.

Jacques introduced the two women, and just as they sat down, two young maids arrived carrying two large trays.

Janine watched wide-eyed as lunch was served: individual molds of tomato aspic and truffles garnished with lemon slices, a platter of sliced roastbeef, turkey, and ham, a basket of hot rolls wrapped in a linen napkin, a watercress salad, a crystal bowl of peaches and cherries, and a bottle of wine in a silver icebucket engraved with a coat of arms. Janine thought the arrangement was as attractive as an illustration in a gourmet magazine.

As Jacques filled their goblets, Janine asked, "Is this from your hothouse grapes?"

"Yes. Do you like it?" he asked with an amused grin. Perhaps he was remembering her description of a wine cooler when he had told her he would have to educate her palate.

She sipped, wrinkling her nose at the tiny bubbles. The bouquet was subtle and the taste smooth and dry. "I love it. It's like champagne."

"Champagne *is* a sparkling wine," said Madame Laurent, looking at Janine with condescension.

Janine said softly, "I thought champagne was . . . champagne."

Madame Laurent said, "That's what happens when the name of a region becomes synonymous with a type of wine. Champagne is the sparkling wine made from the grapes grown in the Champagne region of France."

Jacques cleared his throat and explained, "It's like Kleenex in your country. The word Kleenex has come to mean tissue."

"Oh, yes, Kleenex," said Madame Laurent, dabbing at the corner of one eye with a lace-edged handkerchief smelling of gardenias, "that barbarous American substitute for handkerchiefs. Would you believe that I saw the wife of the United States ambassador pull one out of her purse just last month at the royal ball?"

Janine hoped she would not have to blow her nose in Madame Laurent's presence. She would not have the courage to take a tissue from her pocket.

"Jacques tells me you'll be our guest for a few days, mademoiselle. I hope you find your room comfortable and your stay pleasant." Madame Laurent sounded gracious, but there was a speculative look in her eyes.

"Very comfortable, thank you," Janine replied. Perhaps Madame Laurent didn't know that her niece had no intention of marrying Jacques and she felt that Janine was a threat to Monette.

"Are you having any difficulties adjusting to the food in Brussels?" Jacques asked.

His knee touched hers under the table and Janine smiled at him. "Everything I've eaten has been delicious, and I'm still looking forward to eating mussels. My father loved them, but I've never tasted them."

"I'll have to remedy that," he said. His hand found hers under the table and squeezed it. Madame cleared her throat and looked from one to the other, and Janine pulled away her hand and placed it on the table.

"They're not available in my hometown. Oysters, clams, shrimp, lobsters, and lots of other fresh seafood is flown in regularly, but not mussels."

"I expect that's because they're a rather cheap shellfish, don't you suppose, Jacques?" Madame Laurent cut a dainty piece of roast beef and brought it to her mouth.

Janine felt herself becoming defensive and she toyed with a breadcrumb on the blue tablecloth, squeezing it into a little ball. Almost everything Madame Laurent said seemed a put-down. Was it her imagination, or had the older woman taken an instant dislike to her?

Jacques seemed unaware of any undercurrents and he replied, "That's probably the reason." He turned to Janine and continued, "Mussels are so abundant and inexpensive I assume it isn't worthwhile to pay the air freight from the coast."

Janine had no idea, so she said, "Aunt Laure said that right now they aren't available in Nivelle either. She promised that one of these Mondays, when the café was closed, we'd drive to Ostend to buy some."

"Oh," interjected Madame Laurent, patting her lips with her napkin before sipping her wine. "You must be the little barmaid some of my friends mentioned, the one that works at the Café Central." She raised an eyebrow as she looked at her stepson.

There was no mistake this time. Madame Laurent was being snobbish. Janine had just finished a peach, which suddenly seemed to sit like a rock in her stomach. "Please excuse me, madame, I do hate to eat and run, but," she turned to Jacques, "you said I could use the library, and I want to get started on the article about the Grand' Place."

Jacques looked from Janine to his stepmother and back again, reached across the small table, and, covering Janine's hand with his own, said, "I've selected some books for you. If you wait till I finish my wine I'll show them to you." Then he turned to Madame Laurent, with Janine's hand still imprisoned in his, and said, "Mademoiselle Heerlen came to our country to perfect her French, madame."

Looking from their clasped hands to Jacques's face, Madame Laurent inquired, "In a café?" Her husky voice had a unmistakable undertone of sarcasm.

"What better place? I got to talk to a lot of nice, friendly, unassuming people, who certainly made me feel welcome."

Jacques asked his stepmother, "Do you know Les Alouettes?"

"Yes, of course. That eyesore that should have been torn down ages ago. Why do you ask?"

"It used to belong to Mademoiselle Heerlen's grandfather. Don't you recall?"

Madame Laurent thought for a moment. "Yes, I remember your father mentioning something about his father purchasing it from a certain Monsieur Heerlen, who was in desperate straits." With a languid gesture she reached for some cherries and in so doing a large ruby on her finger captured a ray of sun and splattered bloodred drops of light across the blue tablecloth. "It was so long ago, I had forgotten about Madame Heerlen and those two unfortunate little boys." She turned to Janine and asked, "And you, my dear, are you then the child of one of those poor fellows?"

"I never considered my father a poor fellow, madame, except perhaps at the time of his premature death." Janine stood up. She didn't intend to stay any longer.

Madame Laurent looked satisfied with her performance, and her eyes slid over Janine's jeans and checked blouse. Then she turned to Jacques. "You won't forget the reception at the Royal Palace this afternoon, will you?"

"Of course not," Jacques replied, standing up.

"Thank you very much for your hospitality, Madame Laurent," Janine said without smiling. She turned on her heels and hastened from the garden house.

Jacques dashed after her and tried to take her arm, but she shook herself free and asked, "What have I done to make her dislike me so? Do you suppose she heard me climbing through your window?"

"No, her bedroom is in the other wing. I'm so sorry, Janine. I don't know what possessed her. She's usually so charming."

"I'm certainly glad you didn't tell me it was my imagination."

"Indeed not. Perhaps I should have intervened, but I thought I might make the situation more tense if I did. She behaved inexcusably. I don't know what to say, except to ask you to forgive me for subjecting you to such unpleasantness."

"Let's skip it." She crossed the drawbridge, seeking the safety of her room.

"Janine, please wait." He took her arm and pulled her close to him, and the warmth of his nearness flooded her with the memory of him standing nude on the shore of the pond like a Greek god. "I'll show you the library, if you really mean to do some research."

Walking at his side, she felt all anger and disappointment leave her. It wasn't her fault if Madame Laurent's matchmaking had gone astray, and if the old lady was a snob and didn't approve of her friendship with Jacques, that was her own problem. Janine wouldn't let the woman's sarcasm ruin her day.

Jacques opened the lead-glass door of the square guard tower and ushered Janine into a flagstoned, vaulted chamber. He explained that in ancient times this had been the guardroom, and she imagined Frankish soldiers in leather doublets warming themselves on winter nights around the immense sandstone fireplace. At the peak of the vaulted room were carvings of a sheep and a necklace—the insignias of the Order of the Golden Fleece and the Order of St. Michael. She followed Jacques up a spiral staircase, noticing that the granite steps, worn by centuries of use, dipped slightly in the center.

Jacques opened a massive iron-studded door and escorted Janine into a sunlit room of impressive proportions. Its richness contrasted sharply with the spartan austerity of the guardroom and spiral staircase. The walls were lined by books from floor to ceiling and a ladder on metal runners provided access to all the shelves.

Janine was awed by her surroundings. The library was incredibly luxurious and her eyes darted from the comfortable, modern brown leather chairs to the bouquet of yellow irises in a blue Spode vase on a satinwood table inlaid with tulipwood. Through the tall open windows, Monette's rendition of Revel's "Bolero" drifted into the room with the sun that caressed the mahogany scallop shell at the head of a small couch and the dolphin feet of a tripod table. The furnishings belonged to various periods yet harmonized in an eclectic symphony of textures and colors, and Jacques was the master of it all.

"I love this room. I think I could spend the rest of my life here," she said. The notes of the "Bolero" with their passionate crescendo made her think of Jacques's body moving over hers in the culmination of their union.

She wondered if he could read her mind when he replied, "You'd soon get tired of reading. From my experience and knowledge of you, you don't strike me as a bookworm."

"I like to read, but there are many other things I enjoy as well."

"Yes, I know." The corners of his lips turned up in a crooked grin and his glance traveled over her and lingered on her breasts, then her thighs. She read the memory of the pond in the gray sparkle of his eyes.

She felt the blood rush to her face and walked toward the bookshelves. Running her hand over the spines of some gold-tooled leather bindings, she asked, "Will you tell me where to find the books I need?" She wondered at the impossibility of being just friends with him. Their physical attraction flamed between them like a forest fire and she knew he was exerting all the control in his power not to touch her right now.

He lifted some volumes from the desk and replied, "I've selected these for you and I've placed a marker on the chapters that contain *many* architectural and historical details on the Grand' Place." He approached her and, touching one of the shelves, continued, "If you need other references, here is more material on the same subject."

She felt grateful at the trouble he had taken to help her, but at the same time he had deprived her of ferreting out her own sources, and for her that was one of the most interesting parts of the work. He had even supplied some photographs. "I'm sure the ones you chose will be sufficient. I only intend to write four pages. My editor likes features to be brief." She returned to the desk and leafed through one of the books he had picked for her, unable to read while she could feel his eyes undressing her.

"Yes. I've seen American papers. News and features are sandwiched between advertisements."

"Well, how else can they pay their expenses?"

"And make a profit for their stockholders, no?" He laughed and opened the library door. "I have to go now, but I'll be back soon." His voice held a promise. He stood framed in the open doorway, his blond hair shining like an aura against the shadowy background of the spiral staircase. "On my way out I'll have some coffee sent up to you."

Janine sat at the desk and spread the books on the leather top with its gilded border designs. She took notes on the history and architecture of the Grand' Place until she found her mind wandering.

As if watching a film reel, she reviewed the events that had led to her present emotional state, where the thought of Jacques filled every moment of her waking hours. Her responses to his powerful masculinity had begun like a tiny spark when, hiding among the willow branches, she had first heard his voice with its subtle French burr. Then had come the evening in Brussels, the red rose, the love song he had requested, and his hand caressing her back as they floated with the dance music. But from the minute he had kissed her, she had begun to feel as if she were on a well-oiled slide rushing toward a molten, fiery pit of desire. The moments of passion they had shared in his bed, the lovemaking at the mill, and her consent to undress with him at the willow pond were inexorably leading her to the certainty that she would be his, even if it turned out to be only a brief summer affair. She crossed her arms on the desk and lowered her head into them. Laure's words about class differences and Monette's reiterations of the same subject echoed in her mind. She could have a relationship, if she was willing to let him set her up at Les Alouettes and arrange her life around him. Perhaps he would even marry someone else and keep her secreted at the manor house.

But that wasn't what she wanted. Even a brief affair would be better than that.

She straightened up when she heard a knock on the door and a rosy-cheeked maid brought in a silver tray with coffee and croissants.

"If mam'selle desires anything else, she can please ring the bell," the maid said with a smile. "Does mam'selle wish me to pour her cofeee now?"

"No, thank you," Janine said and looked at her watch. It was nearly five o'clock. "Has Monsieur Laurent returned yet?"

"No. He took his *petite amie* to the Royal Palace." She giggled and covered her mouth with one hand.

"That'll be all, thank you." She smiled to soften the dismissal, but she suddenly realized that she had not heard Monette's music since shortly after Jacques had left her in the library.

After the door closed behind the fresh-faced maid, her words—*petite amie*—kept buzzing around Janine's mind. *Petite amie* didn't just mean "little friend." Janine had always understood it to mean "girl friend." The thought of Jacques making love to Monette the way he had made love to her brought a wave of nausea, and the blood seemed to rush to her ears. Was it possible that, in spite of what Monette had said about Francois, she would get tired of fighting her parents and decide to marry Jacques? Between the two men, there was no doubt in Janine's mind about who was the more attractive and compelling.

She poured coffee from the silver pot into the delicate Limoges cup ard sipped the hot aromatic brew, tasting only bitterness. Jacques hadn't even suggested that she accompany him to the royal reception. How could he take the niece of the owners of a small cafe to such an exalted function? The only place he was willing to assign to her in his life was the hidden, discrete one of mistress, with whom he didn't wish to share his public life.

Laure's words to Pierre echoed in her mind: *He'll use her and discard her, just as if she were a peasant girl.* Janine looked at the luxury of the library furnishings, and through the windows she gazed on the meadows embracing the castle and the shimmering lake. A feeling of hopelessness engulfed her as she recalled her aunt's angry tirade: *He would never, never marry you. You have nothing to offer him but your body."* Her surroundings seemed to bear witness to Laure's statements.

A tiny voice inside her mind seemed to try to revive her hope. Was she going to be defeated so soon? Jacques probably had known Monette all his life and only thought of her as a little sister; and Monette had seemed so open in her determination to marry Francois and hadn't shown any romantic interest in Jacques. She broke off a piece of croissant, buttered it, and chewed it mechanically. It tasted like sawdust. She washed it down with another swallow of coffee and rubbed her temples. She had a splitting headache and all she wanted was to lie down in her room and put Jacques out of her mind.

Gathering up her notes and some photographs Jacques had set out for her, she descended the circular staircase. As she walked through the walled garden, she heard Jacques's and Monette's laughter echoing under the Gothic archway. Rushing to her room, Janine locked her door and threw herself on the bed. She didn't care if she never saw Jacques again.

Six

By eight o'clock Janine had finished typing the article about the Grand' Place and was sitting at her desk watching the swallows cross the purpling eastern sky visible through her open window. As she wondered why Jacques had not sought her out since his return, her musings were interrupted by a knock on her door, and the pounding of her heart told her how eagerly she had waited for him.

When she opened the door, she stepped back and her eyes opened wide in wonder. Jacques, resplendent in full-dress naval uniform adorned with gold braid, stepped into the room carrying a sheaf of papers. The blue sash across his chest and the two heavy gold chains bearing the insignias of the Order of the Golden Fleece and the Order of St. Michael enhanced his aristocratic bearing.

Smiling at her surprise, he said, "Don't let the regalia awe you. Underneath is the body you know, accessible and eager to please." He tried to pull her to him, but she moved out of his reach.

"You look splendid. I'm dazzled," she said, but his appearance only heightened her uncertainties and fears.

"Your words tell me you really go for the uniform, but your actions speak otherwise. What is the matter?"

"I'm tired, that's all." Turning her back to him, she walked to the desk, feeling his eyes boring through her. She stuffed her article and the photographs into a manila envelope, taking more time than necessary to perform the task.

"Then it's time to stop. Dinner is in half an hour and you'll have to dress."

"I was just going to, when you came." Jealousy made her voice sound brittle when she asked, "Where is Monette?" She busied herself closing her portable-typewriter case and wondered if he had spent the hours since his return from the reception in Monette's company. There had been no music issuing from Monette's room for hours.

He threw the papers he had brought onto her desk and, coming up behind her, clasped her about the waist. His teeth nibbled her ear as he replied, "Drinking sherry with madame. I hope you don't prefer her company to mine. I thought you might need some help getting dressed."

His touch and the subtle scent of his aftershave sent a shiver down Janine's spine. Wedged between the desk and his pressing body, for a moment the feel of him made her forget that she wanted to cool off their relationship. But then the thought of his afternoon at the Royal Palace with Monette and her own exclusion from the social event stiffened her resolve. With the gold buttons of his uniform pressing into her back, she leaned forward to avoid the contact just as his hands cupped her breasts.

She suddenly moved her elbows and disengaged herself from his clasp. "I've not needed help with dressing since I was two years old. You're terribly self-centered if you think you're indispensable to me."

"But you are to me. I'm completely centered in you. I was only going to help you choose a dinner dress, unless of course you want me to wash your back." His eyebrow quirked as he watched her and a vaguely ironic smile played about his lips.

"I don't need your help," she snapped, but couldn't help remembering the touch of his hands on her nude body and the caressing look in his eyes as they lay among the yellow weeds of the weeping-willow pond.

He frowned and picked up the papers he had tossed on her desk. "Then all this work was for nothing."

"What is it?"

"Look it over and you'll see."

She thumbed through the papers. In a bold handwriting were all the details she would need for the article on his Missouri vineyard. "You shouldn't have gone to all this trouble, Jacques." There was a constriction in her throat, but it wasn't because she was touched or grateful. She was angry. This was the second time that he had done a portion of her work for her and she felt discounted, as if he thought her incompetent.

"It was no trouble at all. I heard you typing in here and knew you were busy. I deprived myself of your company and made those notes so that we'd have more time together later."

She threw the papers back on the desk and turned about. Leaning against the desk, she supported her weight on her hands and stared at the pale design in the Chinese carpet. She swallowed and said, "I see."

"What is the matter? Why are you upset?" He lifted up her chin while his gray eyes searched her violet ones.

She slapped at his hand and went to open the bedroom door. "Please go and let me get dressed."

Angry in turn, he slammed the door shut and grabbed her arms. As he looked down at her, steely pinpoints stabbed his slate-colored eyes. "Look, let's clear the air right now. I don't like games, and if something is bothering you, I want to know about it. Did my stepmother offend you again while I was in Brussels?"

She shook her head. "It's your notes."

"What do you mean? I thought that was what you wanted." He sounded truly puzzled.

"I wanted an interview. How can I come up with good copy and interesting quotes this way? Shall I inform my readers that my lips taste like Villard Blanc grapes warmed by the sun or that my skin has the bouquet of Leon Millots?

Perhaps they would be interested in the fact that you think I'm like a vineyard ready for harvest."

He threw his head back and laughed. "No, *Chérie. Les Amis du Vin,* true to their name of 'Friends of Wine,' would be beating a path to your door to taste your wonders en masse."

"This is the second time you've done half my work," she said, ignoring his joke. "If you want to write articles, find your own market and stop taking over everything I plan." She tried to free herself, but he held on tightly.

"Pardon me! I'm sorry. I apologize most humbly. I hadn't realized how possessive you are of your work. Believe me, I'll never interfere again." His sarcasm was evident in each staccato syllable that he aimed at her between clenched teeth.

"I'll appreciate that." Her voice was barely audible.

His tone softened. "Janine, I think I understand how you feel. But you were out of sorts when I first entered your room, before you knew what the papers I carried were."

"I already told you. I'm tired and I'm getting more tired by the minute. Let go, you're hurting me." But the hurt really wasn't physical. She wanted to blurt out that it was more painful to dwell on the fact that he hadn't even asked her if she wished to attend the royal reception with him and had taken Monette instead. But how could she? His earlier suggestion that she should move to Les Alouettes, compounded by his not taking her along this afternoon, confirmed her feelings that he was ashamed of her and wanted to keep her hidden away and out of his public life.

His arms went around her and he clasped her close to him and murmured in her hair, "There! There! If you won't tell me, I'll just have to assume that you got upset because I left you alone so long. As I told you, I spent the time writing what I thought you wanted, but I see that I miscalculated. I should have gone with my feelings and joined you as soon as I returned."

His voice was so tender and his embrace so loving that

Janine felt herself melt in his arms and was ashamed of the harsh words she had spoken.

Aware that her resistance and anger were dissolving, he raised her chin and his mouth was gentle and caressing on hers. Her lips opened to his kiss and her arms looped about his neck. With her eyes closed, feeling his body pressed to the length of her own, she remembered how he had looked at the pond earlier in the day, all rippling muscles, sinews, and blond hair.

"That's better," he murmured, and his voice was husky while his hand caressed her back with the same circular motion that had seduced her senses on the dance floor.

"I'd better leave and let you get ready." He released her and she staggered slightly, so lost had she been in his embrace. Steadying her, he said, "I'm afraid that unless I leave immediately, we'll never make it down to dinner. Then madame would send someone up to fetch us." He opened the door and smiled at her.

"I'll see you in a few minutes, Jacques," she replied.

As soon as he left she hurried to her closet and took out a beige dress with tiny brown and orange flowers that featured what was called the "prairie look." The gathered skirt, pinched in at the waist, was mid-calf length and the long sleeves puffed at the shoulder. With the row of tiny buttons that plunged from the high neckline with stand-up collar to the point of the V-shaped bodice that reached her navel, Janine looked petite and demure. She stepped into her brown sling-back heels and thought that if she hadn't left her laced boots at home, she could have passed for an early settler ready to climb aboard a covered wagon. As it was, the illusion was real enough.

As soon as she entered the dining room, she knew that not only had she made the wrong dress choice, but she had nothing in her wardrobe that was suitable for following Jacques's instructions of dressing for dinner.

Ready to sit down at the long tables where silver and crystal sparkled under twin Baccarat chandeliers, Madame Laurent in a long black silk dress with a triple strand of matched pearls as large as hazelnuts looked like a dowager queen; and Monette, in a pale blue floor-length chiffon gown with cap sleeves and a gold-filigree butterfly adorning the modest neckline, looked like the crown princess.

Jacques, very handsome in his dress uniform, smiled at her encouragingly. The three Belgians never batted an eyelash at her American outfit, but Janine felt distinctly uncomfortable and knew that she would either have to buy a dinner dress or dine in her room while she stayed at the chateau.

By the time they finished the chocolate mousse, Janine wondered how she had survived the meal. The conversation had sparkled among the Laurents and Monette while the butler unobtrusively served the various courses. Afterward, the only thing Janine remembered eating were the mussels, which Jacques had ordered especially for her.

All three had tried to draw Janine into the dinner talk, but she had felt uninformed and insular because, ever so subtly, Madame Laurent always managed to turn the conversation to French operas, plays, members of the royal household, and mutual friends. To Janine the dinner had seemed like a showcase for her ignorance.

Seeing her discomfort, when the coffee and liqueurs had been drunk, Jacques asked her to walk in the formal gardens.

"I'm going to retire early tonight, Monette. Why don't you join Jacques and Mademoiselle Heerlen? It's a beautiful moonlight night." Madame smiled at her niece, who promptly consented.

The three of them said good night to Madame Laurent and walked into the walled garden.

As soon as they entered the garden, Monette whispered to Janine, "I have to go and pack the brandy snifters for tomorrow." Then a little louder, to include Jacques, "You two run along. I don't particularly enjoy being the chaperon." She winked at Janine and her taffeta petticoat rustled as she tiptoed to the open french door that led to the upstairs bedrooms.

Janine and Jacques walked across the drawbridge toward the formal gardens and she said, "I'm so sorry I didn't dress appropriately, but I don't have the type of gowns that are required here."

He put his arm about her waist and she leaned her head on his shoulder as they entered the boxwood-edged path where the quarter moon cast rectangular shadows across their feet. "You look beautiful, as you always do."

"You know what I mean. You're just trying to make me feel better."

"I only saw your face, your violet eyes with those dark curving lashes, your dainty hands holding the silverware and toying with the food, and I imagined what the dress covered. I hardly tasted what I ate."

They entered the formal gardens, where the roses and geraniums were pale-scented blurs in the moonlight and statues posed ghost-like within alcoves of greenery. He led her to a white marble bench and pulled her onto his lap. His lips found hers and she opened herself to him while his hand cupped her breast and she felt her nipples respond to his familiar touch. His gold chains were pressing against her side, so she moved her hip to readjust her position.

"You'd better watch out, or have you changed your mind about us being 'just friends'?" He nuzzled her neck, sending a wave of heat from her head to the tips of her toes.

"No, I haven't, even though what we're doing could hardly be classified as the behavior of friends." She ran her fingers through his hair, which felt as soft as spun silk.

"We'll be loving friends, then. Or does 'friendly lovers' sound better?" He began undoing the tiny buttons of her bodice.

She moved his hand and said, "No, Jacques. I thought we agreed that it's too hard on both of us."

His hand crept back to the buttons and he captured her mouth with his. His tongue plundered its inner recesses, and with a flood of feeling that made her blood rush through her veins, Janine remembered his moist caresses as they lay in the golden weeds by the willow pond. With her bodice open to the moonlight and shielded from the soft evening breeze by his warm caress, she called his name, and it was as if she were begging him to take her, make love to her, keep her from retreating once more.

His mouth fastened on her nipple and her fingers searched for an opening inside his jacket. But it was as if the blue sash and the gold buttons and chains armored him against her attempts to touch his skin. With the feel of his uniform under her questing fingers, she remembered her solitary afternoon, and pushing his head away from her bosom, she jumped off his lap. "I said no. What does it take to make you understand? I feel as if I were with an octopus."

"It must be the maritime costume I'm wearing." He stood up and rebuttoned her dress. "I'm afraid I can't keep my hands off you. A second ago I was wishing I had an extra one to hold you still while the other two would play you like a Stradivarius."

He slipped his arm around her waist as they walked through the mazelike gardens, and, wanting his reassurance, she murmured self-consciously, "I'm afraid dinner was a disaster. I never felt so much like an outsider."

"I tried several times to steer the conversation in a direction where you could participate, but you fumbled the ball each time. I thought that when I mentioned quarter horses it'd give you a chance to talk about the American Royal Horse Show."

"But Madame Laurent immediately started asking you about your polo ponies," she remonstrated.

"What about when I began discussing the differences between the American and Belgian educational systems?" he chided.

"By that time I had given up, and, if you remember, she turned to Monette and got her to talk about her boarding school in Switzerland."

"Janine, my stepmother asked you about plays and operas. She was trying to draw you into the conversation." Even though his voice was soft, Janine felt he was getting impatient with her. He was choosing to think that she had withdrawn because she was uninterested and that she was now petulantly placing the blame on his stepmother for her own inability to keep up her end of the dinner talk. Jacques was unaware of how the conversation had been manipulated to make her look uneducated and uninformed.

"Who ever heard of *La Colombe* or *Juana, La Loca?* I've barely heard of *Madame Butterfly!* Can't you see that what happened tonight is the equivalent of what would have happened if Madame Laurent had had dinner at my house and I had talked of bands like Shooting Star and the Clocks?" she snapped.

"The first is a comic opera by Gounod and the second is by Menotti."

She thought she could detect a distinctly patronizing undertone to the information he was imparting. Pushing her elbow into his side, she moved away and hissed, "I don't care if John Philip Sousa wrote them. Without a doubt, Madame Laurent showed off my ignorance and you never even noticed her maneuver."

"I noticed your unresponsiveness," he said harshly, then cleared his throat and said reasonably, "Look, Monette and I knew what madame was talking about and she doesn't know what your education has been. . . ."

"Or lack thereof." She turned about and hurried back toward the boxwood-edged path. "Then go have your conversations with Monette de Turenne and leave me alone!"

The flower-scented summer night had lost all its attraction and Janine was only aware of her hammering heart and feeling of frustration. She was actually having her first real argument with the man she loved—an argument that had really begun when he had come into her room in an effort to help her both with her article and with choosing a dinner dress. Was her jealousy making her unreasonable and coloring all her perceptions? she asked herself.

He caught up with her and whirled her about. "I don't know what is the matter with you, but ever since I came to your room this evening you've been behaving like a porcupine with all its quills sticking out."

"Thanks for the compliment." She tried to free herself, but his hands held her firmly about the waist.

"I'm sorry that the atmosphere at the chateau is uncomfortable for you. What do you say we go to Ostend tomorrow morning? Our villa on the coast is empty and there won't be anyone there to elicit responses of inadequacy from you."

Her bitter laughter echoed from the living walls of the boxwood. She knew she had not been mistaken about Madame Laurent's intent at dinner, and now Jacques was suggesting that her perceptions showed only her inadequacy. Escaping alone with him to a solitary villa on the North Sea coast was ludicrous, and danger signals flashed in her mind. Had he manipulated the dinner debacle so that she, discouraged and distressed, would consent to go with him? "I most certainly will not," she said firmly.

"But I understood you wanted to see Ostend." He lifted her chin and gazed down at her.

The moon reflected silver points in his eyes. "You look like a wolf, and you're beginning to display some of its less-endearing characteristics."

Throwing back his head, he bayed at the moon, and both of them, relieved at the lightening of tension between them, started laughing when a dog from a distant farm howled in response.

"I understand the double meaning of that word, *chérie*, and you must know by now you have nothing to fear from me," he murmured, nuzzling her neck.

A shiver ran through her at the touch of his lips, and she looked up at him with enormous violet eyes. They headed back to the chateau.

"I fear myself, Jacques, more than I fear you," she said, letting him take her hand and breathing deeply with relief as her anger was replaced by a love so deep and encompassing that she wondered how she could have let her fears cloud that one central fact of her relationship with Jacques.

"I'll prove to you tonight that there's no need to worry. I won't come knocking on your door and you'll know just how safe you are." He squeezed her hand and continued with a chuckle, "Of course, my bedroom door will be unlocked so you won't have to climb up the wisteria vine to reach my bed, if you find you're unable to deny your own desires." He stopped in the path and gently nibbled at her ear, sending a thrill of pleasure through her.

She snuggled against him. "I'll hold you to your promise to keep out of my room."

"You have my word." He sighed in mock despair. "Just remember I won't sleep all night and will be lying in my bed listening to every faint noise in the hope you've changed your mind and succumbed to temptation."

"I won't."

"Well then, will you come to Ostend tomorrow, once you know I can be trusted?"

"No," she murmured, shaking her head.

"You're still afraid, little doe?"

"I always am in your presence."

"I'm not your adversary, *chérie*," he reassured her as they crossed the drawbridge. Their steps echoed under the gothic archway.

"Why won't you come away with me and see if we can sort things out?"

Standing in the walled garden surrounded by the perfume of orange blossoms, they gazed at each other, hating to part. He clasped her to him and she could feel the hard length of his body against her own quivering one. She wanted him so much that she wished he would disregard what he had promised, lift her in his arms, and take her to his room. The thought of his hands and lips tracing a delicious course over her bare skin made her tremble with desire. She stepped out of his embrace.

"I might, but not tomorrow." She looked away from his compelling eyes and made an effort to control the quivering of her voice when she said, "I told Uncle Pierre I'd see him in the morning." The words sounded inane in the midst of the storm raging through her entire being. "Good night, Jacques." She kissed him lightly on the lips and hurried upstairs to her room.

In the morning, when Monette parked her blue Renault before the Café Central, Janine thought the village square would burst at the seams. Row after row, every kind of portable stall covered the cobblestones. Music, laughter, shouts, and haggling filled the air. Shoes, dresses, garden produce, cooking utensils, chimes tinkling in the breeze, and even puppies and kittens changed hands. Open vans sold cheeses, fried potatoes—the famous Belgian *frites*— and *charcuterie*—pink hams and red salami from the Ardennes, which filled the air with their spicy aroma.

Pierre Heerlen was helping several farmers bring out their stalls from the old garage behind the café where they had been stored all week. As soon as he was through, he and Francois, slender, dark-haired, and vaguely melancholic, set up a long folding table in a space the young man had reserved among the other booths while he waited for Monette's arrival.

Within half an hour the three young people had arranged the brandy snifters on the table and Monette had poured in the water at various levels to achieve the proper sounds. Monette was dressed in her red gypsy skirt and was wearing large hoop earrings, which looked rather incongruous with her straight blond hair and her pixie face. When she began her concert with a spirited rendition from *Aïda*, a circle formed around her and soon coins began to fall in the open guitar case on the ground by the table.

By noon there was a sizable amount of cash in the case, and just as the young woman started to play a popular French song, accompanied by the rhythmic clapping of the spectators, Madame Laurent and her gray-uniformed chauffeur hurried to the site of the performance.

"Pagnol, you may empty the water from the glasses," Madame Laurent ordered.

The chauffeur, looking tight-lipped and uncomfortable,

poured out the water, which splattered onto the cobblestones, and began packing the glasses in the cardboard boxes Monette had stored under the table.

"But I'm not through with my concert," Monette wailed.

"Oh yes you are," said Madame Laurent, turning the guitar case upside down and emptying the money onto the cobblestones. The coins rolled in every direction and the circle of spectators stepped back. There were murmurings and giggles, which stopped suddenly when Monette started sobbing.

Madame Laurent squeezed her niece's arm and pulled her toward the silver Mercedes parked before the shuttered schoolhouse. As she passed Janine, who was staring at the pavement in embarrassment, she hissed, "This may be appropriate behavior where you come from, Mademoiselle Heerlen, but it certainly won't do here. I'm afraid you are a negative influence on my niece, so, as long as Jacques insists on keeping you at the chateau, I guess I'd better return her to her parents."

Janine flinched, but before she could answer, Monette said, "She had nothing to do with it." Tears were running down the girl's face as she disappeared into the Mercedes while Pagnol loaded the boxes and guitar case in the trunk.

Francois had stood back during the confrontation, a helpless expression on his face. Monette had been forbidden to see him and the young man was in no position to intervene in his girl friend's behalf without making matters worse for her.

After he and Pierre took the folding table back to the café, he asked Janine doubtfully, "Do you want a ride back to the chateau?"

Janine shook her head. Jacques was in Nivelle and there was nothing she wanted less than being at the mercy of Madame Laurent. "What about Monette's car?" she asked, trying to decide what she should do.

"Don't worry about it. They'll send somebody after it," Francois replied bitterly.

Janine felt discouraged and somehow soiled by the

scene. Madame Laurent's words had been so low that none of the spectators could have heard her, but her actions had spoken more loudly than if she had shouted, and people were watching her and Francois with a mixture of pity and amusement, while children scrambled to collect the discarded coins.

"If you don't mind riding on my motorscooter, would you like to go to Waterloo with me?" Francois asked, apparently wanting to get away from Orpe Le Petit as much as she did.

"I'd like that very much," Janine replied.

The Vespa backfired when Francois started it, and Monsieur Charcot, the Laurents' agent, who had stood watching from a distance, teased the young man, "When are you going to get the exhuast fixed, Monsieur Beaumont? I keep thinking the Germans are shooting up the town once more." The pale blue eyes in the ruddy face of the plump, middle-aged man were friendly, and he seemed to be trying to distract Francois from the recent unpleasantness.

"I'm working on it, Monsieur Charcot. I'll solve the problem one of these days."

The Vespa backfired again and Janine, sitting behind Francois with her arms around his waist, turned to wave to Laure and Pierre, who were standing in the doorway of the café with their hands over their ears and an embarrassed expression on their faces.

Janine and Francois bounced along the highway between Orpe and Waterloo. Within ten minutes, the lion-crowned, grass-covered pyramid commemorating Napoleon's defeat towered above them.

After climbing several hundred steps, they leaned across the wrought-iron railing at the foot of the white-marble lion atop the monument and tried to catch their breath while they gazed at the historical battleground spread at their feet.

A hawk overhead glided in ever-widening circles and Janine remembered her ride from the mill to the pond at Jacques's side. Did he love her? she wondered. Surely if he did he would have told her by now. Peering into the distance, she said, "From here all the villages look alike. Is that Orpe Le Petit?" she asked, gazing to the east and wondering what Jacques would have done if he had witnessed the events at the fair. Would he have taken his stepmother's side as he had done the night before? Monette's request that she keep their plans secret surely meant that Jacques wouldn't have approved of the undertaking.

"No," Francois replied, pointing to the southeast. "Over there. Don't you see the Laurents' chateau?"

Janine blinked against the glare of the overcast day and saw the castle looking like a toy in the middle of its lake. "Did you hear what Madame Laurent said to me?" she asked.

"Yes, but don't take it to heart. It was just a matter of time before she interfered with Monette and me, and you just provided the convenient excuse."

"Where do her parents live? Will it be too far for you to drive to see her?"

Francois shook his head. "It's not so much the distance to her house. She lives close enough, just on the outskirts of Liège, but I'm afraid they'll send her out of the country so I won't be able to see her anymore."

"It'll be hard to be parted, but when she turns twenty-one you can get married."

"No, Janine, I'm not going to do that. I love her very much and lately I've come to realize that it wouldn't be fair to her. She's used to luxuries I could never provide and our backgrounds are so dissimilar that she would soon start being ashamed of me and hating me. I can't face that. She'd be much better off married to Jacques Laurent."

"But she seems determined to become your wife." Janine kept her tone even, but she wanted to grab Francois and shake him so he'd hurry and explain Jacques's and Monette's relationship to her.

"In the aristocracy of this country, the older generation has all the power. The young might kick, scream, and rebel, but in the end they submit," Francois said with a catch in his voice.

"But she doesn't love Jacques. The most you can say is that they're friends."

"She likes him well enough, and with me out of the way she'll soon learn to love him."

To hide her hurt and fear at his prediction, Janine walked around the base of the lion's statue. Returning to Francois's side, she asked, "What about him? I don't think he's in love with her, either."

"Love has nothing to do with it. The marriage would be the joining of two old wealthy families. Did you know that Monette is the godchild of the royal princess and that Jacques is related to all the royal houses of Europe? He has no title because one of his ancestors died without male issue. His great-grandmother was the last direct descendant of the dukes of Bourgogne, and when she married, the title was lost, but the estate remained in the family. That's how aristocratic families increase their holdings—through marital alliances."

Janine's heart seemed to skip a beat and she felt as if an unfillable, gaping hole had taken its place in her breast. A shiver went through her and she turned up the collar of her blazer. What was the matter with her? She had already glimpsed the reasons for the impossibility of a serious commitment from Jacques, and her poor performance at dinner had underlined her inadequacies. But she knew now that her determination to guard herself had already weakened and that last night she had wanted Jacques more than she had ever wanted anything in her life. Had she no pride? she angrily asked herself. Her words caught in her throat and she cleared it before asking, "Do you think they'll get engaged?"

Francois hit the rail with a clenched fist and a metallic sound reverberated along the enclosure. The vibration lingered like a dirge to her hopes. He said between clenched teeth, "They'll soon be, probably before the end of summer. At least if it's up to the de Turennes and Madame Laurent.

But in a few days I'm going to France to visit my grandparents, and there are definite possibilities that I'll find a position where they live. At least I'll not be around to witness the festivities."

"Neither will I," Janine whispered, more to herself than to her downcast companion.

"We'd better go now," the young man said, and hurried down the steep flight of stairs.

Janine dashed after him, her thoughts still in turmoil, and caught up with him halfway down the stairs. Her hand on the cold metal railing, she avoided looking at him when she said, more to cheer herself than to reassure him, "Till they marry, nothing's certain."

He nodded but looked disconsolate as he said, "I won't deprive her of her birthright, Janine. Neither will I put myself in a position where she'll feel as if she has to apologize for me. If she doesn't marry Laurent, she'll marry somebody else who belongs to her class. I won't stand in her way and make her life or my own miserable."

On the ride back to Orpe Le Petit, Janine leaned her head against Francois's shoulders, using him as a shield. After the windswept chill of the lion monument, the sun was pleasant on her back and the warmth of his body was comforting.

It was apparent to her that European upper-class customs were different from those at home, and love didn't seem to conquer all. Family and financial consideration were more important than romantic love. From the conversation with Francois she deduced that, if it came to pass, Monette's and Jacques's would be a marriage of convenience; but who could say what type of marriage would be the most enduring—one where the couple was very much in love, or one where the match was arranged by the families? In many parts of the world, marriages were alliances that joined financial interests. In the United States, people married for love, yet the divorce rate was the highest in the world.

The Vespa hit a chuckhole and backfired. Janine tightened her grip around the young man's waist. She knew that she couldn't marry without love and she intended her marriage to last for her entire life. That was why she had never even been close to making a commitment. The thought of intimacy without love had always been repulsive to her. But now, for the first time in her life, she felt almost overpowered by her attraction to a man. The confines of her own being had seemed to blur and dissolve so that, in order to grow and be complete, she wanted to be joined to the only man she had ever loved. Her emotions were fighting a winning battle against her reason, and Jacques was the danger before which all her resolves seemed to surrender.

A truck passed them and the Vespa swerved toward the shoulder of the highway. The diesel fumes overpowered the smell of clover, warm and heavy in the air. Laure's words reverberated in Janine's mind: *Do you think he'll marry you?* Till those words had been spoken, in spite of her attraction, Janine had not even thought of marrying Jacques. Unwittingly, Laure had planted the seed, which had germinated and become as huge as a jungle tree in an incredibly brief span of time. The answer, unacknowledged even to herself, had been: *Why not?* She had had brief glimpses of the impossibility of their union, and Francois had put her own doubts into words when he had given her the reasons why he couldn't marry Monette.

The young man turned into the now-deserted village square of Orpe Le Petit just as the barrier was lowered for an approaching train. Over the noise of metal against metal and the Vespa's roar, he turned his head and shouted, "Please don't mention what I said."

"I won't," she promised as the train disappeared in the distance and the barrier lifted.

They arrived at the chateau in the late afternoon, and, in spite of all her fears, she was eager to see Jacques. He was always able to soothe away her worries, and in his presence, with his arms about her and the velvety caress of his gray eyes, he seemed the only important thing in her life.

When she reached her room, she found two large white

cardboard boxes on her bed and over them a note in Jacques's bold handwriting. She tore open the envelope and was engulfed by disappointment when she read:

Chérie,

Early this afternoon I suddenly had to leave for London, where I'll spend a couple of days. I wanted to take you with me, but couldn't find you anywhere. Monette and Madame Laurent had already left for Liege without a word of explanation and no one at the chateau or at the café seemed to know where you were. I'm sorry. As soon as I return, we're going to Ostend and I'll not take no for an answer. I hope you like the dinner dresses I bought for you. They'll replace the clothes I helped destroy during our lively encounters.

Yours,
Jacques

Seven

Two days later, at ten o'clock in the morning, Janine and Jacques were driving to Ostend.

Janine was thinking how handsome he looked in his navy blazer and gray slacks and how much she had missed him during his brief absence, when he echoed her thoughts by remarking, "I could hardly wait to come back from London." He reached for her hand and brought it to his lips.

"I wondered if you were having a good time with some British debutante," she replied. She knew she looked attractive in her white dress—the double collar edged with eyelet spread like a shawl over the shoulders of her waist-length burgundy jacket and delicately framed her face—yet she felt she couldn't compete with the wealthy, elegant women who moved in Jacques's circles.

He laughed. "I went to buy a prize bull. He'd hardly qualify as a debutante. Your jealousy is a compliment, but have you already forgotten that I wanted to take you with me? Didn't you find my note?"

"Yes, I did. And thank you for the lovely dinner gowns," she said.

"I envy the silk they're made of. It'll touch your body and caress your skin."

"Not as softly as your hands," she murmured.

He smiled at her and rubbed the nape of her neck, sending a well-remembered thrill down her spine. They rode quietly for several miles, then she told him of the incident at the village fair.

Jacques frowned and remarked, "You and Monette had a very odd idea in giving a public performance. I can imagine that my stepmother was appalled."

She stared at the distant medieval towers and spires of Bruges, dreamlike in the morning haze, and said, "I feel as if you're ashamed of me."

The Jaguar swerved slightly, and he gripped the steering wheel. "What did you just say?" he asked incredulously.

"You chose to take Monette to the reception." Her voice was so soft it was barely audible over the hum of the engine.

"Chose? Oh, now I know what was the matter with you the other evening." He sighed impatiently. "I'm sorry, but I keep forgetting you don't know our customs. I couldn't take you to the royal palace because you weren't invited. The only reason I escorted Monette was because she also had an invitation and happened to be a guest at the chateau. If I'd met you a couple of weeks earlier, and had known you wanted to go, I could've arranged it."

"I thought . . . Jacques, are you going to marry her?" Janine blurted. She'd been thinking about Francois's remarks ever since Waterloo.

He shook his head and said, "I hope this nonsense won't ruin our trip. I'd counted on picking up where we left off, but it seems that for every step forward we take two backward. You must have a poor opinion of me. Do you really think I'm planning to marry her while I make love to you?"

Janine bit her lip and didn't reply. He'd answered her question with another question.

They were now skirting Bruges, and he changed the subject by telling her about the decline of the ancient city whose prosperity had plummeted after the silting over of the Zwin River. Then he added, "Of course, it's more complex than that, just like everything else."

Janine wondered if he was referring to their own relationship or to himself and Monette. Their conversation continued with long pauses between desultory remarks, and the undercurrents between them were almost palpable in the close confines of the car.

When the sea appeared on the horizon, she said, "Once I saw a painting of a Belgian fisherman on horseback. Do they still fish that way?"

"Yes. That's how they drag for shrimp. We'll drive along the coast and you can watch them. It's quite picturesque." He was quiet for a moment, then added softly, "The North Sea is cruel and unpredictable, just like a young woman I know."

While they were talking they'd arrived in Ostend and were now driving along the broad waterfront boulevard. Dozens of hotels, built in the style of the previous century, with wide porches framed by intricate scrollwork, faced the sea, and tourists strolled leisurely along the promenade atop the dike.

Jacques parked by the yacht harbor, where sailboats, pleasure cruisers, and fishing vessels bobbed at anchor or headed toward the open sea. There was a smell of fresh fish, and the air had a briny, invigorating tang. Gulls screeched and circled in the overcast sky. A cobblestoned causeway stretched to a distant pier that marked the entrance of the commercial port. Along the causeway, crowds milled around tables shaded by colorful patio umbrellas.

"Is that the fish market?" she asked, caught up in the bustle and festive air.

"Yes. We can walk through it if you wish."

She had never seen such a variety of fresh seafood. There were soles and flounders, cods and herrings, oysters and clams packed in seaweed, and she watched a fishwife, every roll of her heavy torso outlined by a brightly striped T-shirt, wrap several pounds of baby octopuses in newspapers and place them in a plastic bag for a customer.

"They look harmless enough," Jacques teased, following her gaze.

"That's because they're dead," Janine said with a smile,

remembering their exchange in the chateau's gardens, when he'd wished he possessed an extra arm.

They retraced their steps and Janine observed several people standing around a parked van. Through a side window of the vehicle, the owner of the mobile restaurant was doing a brisk business selling tiny boiled shrimps and fried potatoes, which the customers ate as they walked along the promenade.

The spicy smell made Janine's mouth water, and Jacques smiled at her and said, "I'd thought we'd eat a sole almondine at the Prince Albert in about an hour, but from the look on your face I'd guess you're hungry for *crevettes.*"

His gray eyes were devouring her, and she felt herself tremble in anticipation of the promise they held. The promise had nothing to do with a meal. "I can wait," she said, wanting to leave the crowded boulevard and feel his arms about her once again.

Jacques squeezed her arm and grinned at her. "There go all my plans for an elegant luncheon. We'll picnic on the beach instead."

Walking with him on the tawny sands sounded as appealing as cutting school on the first day of warm weather. Then suddenly she realized how disappointed she was feeling because he'd not mentioned the villa, either during the drive or since their arrival. Perhaps he didn't intend to take her there after all. While he'd been away, all her thoughts had been of him and of the brief time they still had together before she would have to return home. She knew now that she couldn't bear to think of leaving without belonging to him completely. Certain that a summer romance was all she could hope for, she told herself that she'd settle for that, and the memory would nourish and sustain her later.

With a catch in her voice, she answered, "Whatever you decide is all right with me."

He quirked an eyebrow and asked, "Are you putting yourself in my hands?" His lips brushed her temple, and she looked up at him. Her eyes lingered on his mouth, and she wanted to kiss him, not caring about the passers-by.

"I've been in your hands ever since I met you," she whispered. Then she made a feeble joke, in an attempt to dispel the mounting tension between them. "So long as you don't suggest we go swimming."

Jacques leaned on the railing and looked down at some children wading and splashing in the shallow waters. "Perhaps that's what I need right now—a plunge in that cold sea."

Her hand barely touched his on the railing, and she wished she had the courage to say, *You won't need to do that, not if you still want me.* Instead, she pointed to a ship partially hidden by a distant pier. "That's odd. I've been watching that ship for several minutes. Its prow is aimed toward the open sea, but it seems to be entering the harbor backward."

"Sometimes one has to go at things in a roundabout way. But you're seeing correctly. That's the ferry from Dover. The entrance is so narrow that it backs in, then it doesn't have to turn around."

When he circled her waist and held her close, her heart began to beat faster. They hadn't kissed in two days, and she wanted to be alone with him, to feel his lips on hers, and to run her hands on his bare skin, but he didn't seem inclined to hurry.

"Ostend is the railhead for the rest of the Continent. Also, the London–Istanbul highway begins here. What else would you like to know?"

She could tell from the soft, caressing look in his gray eyes that this wasn't the only knowledge he wished to share.

He guided her to a park bench near the railing and said, "We'll drive along the coast and find a spot for our picnic."

"That's not the way to Istanbul, is it?" she joked.

He laughed. "We won't need to go that far. The mysteries of that city aren't any more fascinating than the mystery of you. Wait here and I'll get our lunch."

In a short while the Jaguar pulled up at the curb, and Janine hurried to join Jacques. As they proceeded along the coastal highway, Janine looked from the sea on her right to the fields on her left and said, "It's awesome to think that these seawalls are the only defense."

"Sometimes a thin wisp of silk or the human will are a stronger defense than granite," Jacques replied, staring straight ahead.

The stone slope changed to sand covered by high coarse grass, which waved gently in the northeasterly breeze. The gray sea lapped the tawny shore in low swells and at the horizon blended with the leaden sky. The sand and the grass were the only touches of color in the panorama.

They passed a shuttered, white-stucco villa surrounded by wind-twisted pines and a wrought-iron fence, and Jacques said, "That's our summer house. My father and I used to spend two months there every summer. I've a very pleasant recollection of those days." He looped his arm about her shoulders and murmured, "Perhaps today will supplant all my childhood memories."

Janine watched the villa disappear behind a sand dune. He did intend to take her there after all, and his touch and the anticipation of being alone with him in the empty house sent shivers through her. The intrusive thought that he might be in the habit of bringing all his girl friends to this isolated spot made her catch her breath. She sat up straighter and asked, "Do you come here often?"

"My father and his wife come for the regatta in August and sometimes spend a week or so when they want to go to the Wellington racetrack. I stay there while I take part in the international jumping tournaments." He hesitated. "Once in a while, when I feel the need to be alone, I spend a few days just walking along the beach, sailing, or fishing. It renews me." He ruffled her hair and smiled. "But if you're asking me whether I've brought another woman here, the answer is no."

Janine smiled and leaned back against the soft red leather seat. She felt as if she and Jacques were one with the sky and the sea and the gulls wheeling overhead. In the distance, the triangles of several sailboats seemed to mirror the white of the gulls' wings. She looked at his handsome profile, and her love for him engulfed her. She was ready to give herself to him, yet fingerlike tendrils of apprehension tensed her thigh muscles.

Jacques stopped on the shoulder of the highway and said, "Let's have our picnic now. I've been famished since I bought the *crevettes.*"

From the trunk of the Jaguar he extracted a covered wicker basket, and they walked hand in hand down the steep grassy embankment toward the fine golden sands. The breeze whipped Janine's dress against her body, molding it to her legs, and she stopped a moment to remove her sling-back wedges, which had filled with sand.

On the beach, with a satisfied *"Voilà!"* he spread a white-linen tablecloth and began laying out their provisions.

"Let me help you," she offered. Then, looking inside the hamper, she asked, "Where did you get all this?" Besides the shrimp and fried potatoes, there were crisp rolls, a bottle of wine, grapes, silverware, glasses, and china.

Jacques grinned. "I bought the food you wanted from the street vendor, as you seemed to have your heart set on that. Don't you know by now that I'm eager to grant your every wish?" He kissed her lightly on the lips. "But I obtained the rest from the maître d' at the Prince Albert Hotel."

After the tasty meal and crisp, dry wine, they walked on the hard-packed sand near the edge of the water, and Janine picked up a seashell and stopped to study its perfection. The inside was pale lilac shading to purple, and the convex exterior was a delicate beige-and-brown plaid pattern.

As she held it in her palm, he rubbed the outside of the shell with his thumb and said, "It's the shape of your breast. Exquisite." His thumb trailed along her wrist and a shiver crept up her arm. He turned the shell over and added, "The deeper shade of violet is the color of your eyes, so deep and soft at the same time. Do you collect seashells?"

"No. I just thought this one'd remind me of today." She put the shell in her pocket.

"I won't need a souvenir to remind me." He turned her to face him. His gray eyes, compelling and caressing like the waves lapping the shore, looked into the deep violet depths of hers, and he pulled her to him. His arms encircled her, and his hands molded the swell of her hips against the hardness of his body.

Her knees felt weak and unable to sustain her weight while her heart pounded in her breast as if it were ready to leap out of her rib cage. Clasping her arms about his neck, she said, "I even dream of you at night, and when I wake up in the morning I feel as if you'd just left my side."

"You can make your dreams reality, *chérie,*" he said with a catch in his voice.

Closing her eyes, she lifted her face to him, her lips open to his compelling need. For a long moment, he kissed her gently but fully upon her mouth. Then his hands moved to her waist, and his lips traveled slowly to her eyes and hair, sending a thrill of desire crawling over her skin.

She lost all consciousness of time and place. The only sound was the blood rushing through her veins, and the beating of his heart against her own. The pounding surf seemed to have melded with their being in a primordial, powerful cadence to which their heated bodies responded with every primitive instinct.

When he let her go, she held on to his arm to steady herself. For a moment she was disoriented and blinked and looked about to get her bearings. The Jaguar looked like a red toy in the distance, and in the opposite direction, just rounding a dune, two fishermen on horseback advanced slowly toward them. She realized they were the reason why Jacques had released her. Near their feet, the sea licked the sand, and a drop of water spattered on her face.

Jacques, his hand cradling her neck, rubbed the drop from her cheek and said huskily, "It's starting to rain. We'd better go to the villa now."

Running along the shore, they laughed as the rain

increased in intensity. There was no way to make it back to the car without getting drenched. At Jacques's concern, she replied, "Don't worry. I'm all wash and wear."

By the time they reached the Jaguar, they were panting. The rain was coming down in sheets, and Janine felt as if she'd been running under a waterfall. Their wet clothes clung to their bodies, and puddles formed on the car seats and carpet.

Chilled through and through, her soaking hair streaming rivulets down her face, Janine sneezed.

"I hope you don't catch cold. In a couple of minutes I'll get you dry and warm you up," Jacques said as he sped toward the villa.

The sea was no longer visible through the curtain of rain, and the windshield wipers were ineffective against the torrential onslaught. The villa seemed like a haven in the rainstorm, but another storm, more powerful than the elements, raged inside Janine.

He preceded her through the darkness of the shuttered rooms, turning on lights as he advanced. The furniture, covered by white dustsheets, created an eerie, secretive atmosphere, and the subtle, clean odor of cedar and camphor pervaded the house.

Jacques led Janine into a luxurious bathroom with a large blue-tiled sunken tub and mirror-covered walls. Her teeth chattering from the cold, she watched him turn on the hot water.

"Come on, *chérie*, let's get your clothes off," he said, unbuttoning her jacket. He turned her about and unzipped her dress, which joined the jacket on the tiled floor.

She stepped out of her panties and unclasped her bra while he adjusted the temperature of the water and poured in a generous amount of bath salts from a silver and crystal bottle on the edge of the tub. The mirrors about them reflected her nude body to infinity.

"In you go," he said, pulling her by the arm and helping her into the tub.

Soaking in the perfumed water, she watched him shivering from the cold as he stripped off his wet clothes with quick movements. His beautifully shaped limbs covered by curling blond hair and his undisguised maleness were tremendously arousing to her. A surging need for intimate contact dispelled the last trace of chill from her blood, and when he joined her in the water, she found that her breath was coming in tiny gasps.

The scented steam filling the bathroom made her feel as if they were floating through a warm, dreamlike mist. When he pulled her close to him, she snuggled her face between his neck and shoulder, feeling his hard length against her.

He stroked her wet satiny body, and they floated against each other, buoyed by the fragrant water. "You're so lovely, Janine," he murmured with a catch in his voice. He caressed her breasts, and her erect nipples delighted at his touch.

When he lifted her over him, his gray eyes soothed her fears and promised pleasure. His eagerness, evident in every taut muscle of his body, set her senses reeling as he guided her hips against him.

"Can you feel how much I want you?" he asked, his voice low and urgent. Not waiting for a response, he drew her face to his. His lips found hers, and his kiss soon changed from gently probing to sensuously compelling.

She parted her lips, and his tongue suggestively searched the depths of her mouth, while his hands pressed her hips to him. Feeling her legs float apart above him, lost in the heat that swamped all her senses, she reached around his shoulders and pushed herself against him. Captured by their feelings, they clutched each other and slid underwater.

They came up spluttering. Grabbing her under her arms, he sat her up facing him. They laughed together, but when their eyes met, the laughter died in their throats.

Cupping her face in his hands, he looked at her for a moment, then pushed her hair away from her forehead with a tender gesture and said, "Come on, *chérie*, let's get dry."

She nodded, unable to answer.

He stepped out of the tub and stretched his hand out to her.

She took it and stepped out of the water, which puddled about her feet and darkened the carpet. He enveloped her in a terrycloth bath sheet as soft and luxurious as velvet. While she dried her hair with a corner of the towel, he applied friction to her back and arms, then turned her about and gently began drying her breasts and stomach.

Then it was her turn to dry his back. When he turned around, he let his bath sheet fall open and enveloped her in it so that his naked body pressed against her.

She let her towel drop to the floor and ran her fingers through the blond hair of his chest and nuzzled his nipples, her lips soft and her tongue teasing.

She wanted him right this moment and wished he'd lift her in his arms and take her to his bed. Instead he took a blue velour robe from the mirrored bathroom closet and slipped her arms into the sleeves. Then he kissed her lips lightly and said, "Mm, you taste delicious."

"It must be the bath salts," she said, hugging the long robe about her and tying the belt. She felt disappointed that she was covered up once again.

"I'll make a fire in the fireplace and put your clothes in the dryer. Then we'll have a little glass of cognac. We can't take a chance on you catching a chill."

"With you around there's no chance of that," she murmured, following him to the living room and wondering if he had decided not to make love to her.

With his white bath sheet draped around him like a toga, Jacques kneeled before the fieldstone fireplace and lighted the kindling under the stacked logs. Then with quick, purposeful gestures, he swept the dustsheets off the furniture, revealing deep, comfortable sofas and chairs in soft beiges and browns.

A wide window faced the dunes and the sea, while the torrential rain designed wavering waterfalls across the expanse of glass. The sea, the sky, and the rain blended in all shades of gray and enveloped the house in a moist cocoon, while the surf pounding against the beach and the pine trees swaying in the storm played an accompaniment to the crackling, leaping fire.

Jacques left the room, and Janine sat on a mound of cushions before the fireplace. The fire seemed to echo the heat of the blood rushing through her veins. He had said he'd put her clothes in the dryer. Was he planning to take her back to the chateau as soon as the rain stopped and her dress dried? Even in the tub he had shown remarkable restraint, more so than he had at the pond. Perhaps he had decided that, since she'd said she didn't want to give herself to him without a commitment on his part, and he wasn't ready for that, he wouldn't approach her again. But she wanted to belong to him entirely, even if it was just for a few days.

Now, after all her previous refusals, she would somehow have to let Jacques know she'd changed her mind. How would she do that, unless he tried to make love to her and she didn't push him away?

When he rejoined her, he'd changed into jeans and a light blue sportshirt and dried his hair so that it framed his face like a golden aura. He walked to a sideboard near the window and from a crystal decanter poured cognac into two brandy snifters.

"I guess every time I see one of those glasses I'll think about the ill-fated concert in the village square," she said. She couldn't bring herself to mention Monette again, and she wrapped her arms around herself at the sudden tremor that went through her. Perhaps, when Madame Laurent had taken Monette back to her parents, Jacques had realized he'd miss her.

At the mention of the fair, he shook his head as one does about a childish prank, then handed Janine her cognac. "Drink this now," he said and joined her on the cushions.

The fiery liquid brought tears to her eyes and made her

cough. "It's too strong. I don't think I can drink it," she said, snuggling up to him.

He nibbled her earlobe and said, "Do what the doctor's ordering. It'll warm you, since you're so reluctant to let me do the job." His hand caressed her ankle and crept up to her knee. He stopped there.

Holding very still, she wondered what she should do next. Should she unfasten the belt of her robe so that he'd know she wasn't holding back? She swallowed the rest of her cognac and waved her hand before her burning lips.

Taking her glass from her, he placed it on the hearth together with his own, then his arm circled her shoulders and he eased her back among the cushions.

She closed her eyes and abandoned herself to the feel of his lips in the hollow of her neck, in her hair, on her eyelids. His tongue traced the shell-like outline of her ears, sending fingers of pleasure arrowing across every inch of her skin. She sighed with pleasure and relief. How foolish she'd been to think he didn't want to make love to her!

With his warm breath mingling with hers, he whispered her name and murmured of nights they could spend here and at the chateau, and of trips together.

She hardly heard his endearments, so lost was she in the grip of her sensations. The pleasure he'd given her in the golden bower by the willow pond was like a remembered taste, and now she wanted all of him and craved to feel the power of his masculine body take complete possession of her.

"Jacques, oh, Jacques." His name escaped her lips like a sob.

His mouth found hers, and he kissed her hungrily while inside her robe his hand caressed and cradled her responding breasts. Her erect nipples had ached for his touch, and she moaned and clasped him about the shoulders so fiercely that he could barely move.

He unfastened the belt of her robe and looked at her. "Your body's like ivory against the blue velvet," he said. His voice, husky in her ears, questioned, pressed, demanded, and she abandoned herself to the tempest of her feelings, which seemed to echo the storm raging outside.

She reached for the buttons of his shirt, but his own impatient fingers took over, and he stripped off his clothes as he knelt by her. With the fire at his back, his body looked incandescent around the edges, and she stretched her arms toward him.

He swept her up in his arms and took her to his bedroom, while her face nestled in his neck, and she inhaled the warm scent of him.

The bedcovers were already turned down, and when he laid her gently on the cool white sheets, she realized that he had known all along they were going to make love.

"I thought you didn't want me anymore," she said with a sound of anticipation in her voice.

In the dusky grayness of the bedroom, he climbed onto the bed and gently parted her legs. Kneeling between them, his eyes never left hers. "You'll never know how close I came to taking you against your will. That's why I told you that the human will is stronger than granite." His hands traveled the length of her body, lingering on her breasts, on her heaving abdomen, along her thighs.

She felt a weakness engulf her and closed her eyes. But behind her closed eyelids she could still see his broad shoulders, his body covered by fine gold hair, and his powerful throbbing maleness eager to claim her. "Oh, Jacques! Why did you make me wait so many hours?"

"I wanted you to be ready for me, sweetheart. I was afraid you'd push me away again, and this time I wouldn't have listened to you. You're like a living work of art. I'll never get enough of you," he said huskily.

"And I of you," she whispered. She opened her glazed eyes and looked at him, and it was as if he were enveloped in a mist.

His eyes were gentle and demanding at the same time, and, unable to sustain his gaze, she pulled his head down. His lips fastened on hers in a long kiss that seemed to drink her very essence. Then his hands wended a course over her neck and her breasts, her abdomen, and his mouth followed with moist, seductive, lingering kisses that sent throbbing shivers coursing down her spine.

Janine's surroundings receded and her breath came in gasps. Was he going to take her to the pinnacle of sensation as he had done at the willow pond and not complete their union? His tongue was tracing a moist, wicked path along her inner thighs, when she felt a shudder begin to claim her, and she grabbed his hair and pulled his head up. "Take me, Jacques! Please!" she entreated, feeling as if her body were molten wax dissolving under him.

His eagerly sought weight pressed on her. The sudden pain made her whimper on a released, labored breath. Jacques hesitated and, lifting himself up on his elbows, looked down at her in wonder. *"Chérie! Chérie!* I didn't know!"

She arched her writhing body to meet his and grasped his buttocks in a frenzy of desire and fear that he'd stop now, when he was all she wanted or would ever want.

For a moment he kissed her lips tenderly, almost chastely, then his hardness plumbed her very depths, and she moaned, not in pain but in exquisite pleasure, forgetting everything but the peak where he took and kept her for exquisitely long moments. Entwined, their feelings and their bodies were joined and melted in complete union.

When he lifted himself off, he lay at her side. He slipped an arm under her shoulders and a leg over hers so that she was cradled in his embrace. His hand moved along her body with a soft tracery of caresses, and his voice was tender and soft with pleasure when he asked, "How do you feel, sweetheart?"

"Happy, fulfilled, contented." She snuggled closer to him and hid a yawn in his neck. "And sleepy."

He ran his fingers through the damp tendrils of dark hair clinging to her forehead and pulled the covers over them just as a bolt of lightning illuminated the twilit room, and was immediately followed by a clap of thunder that shook the room and reverberated with booming echoes.

Startled, she tensed against him, and he hugged her in a closer embrace, murmuring reassurances as she fell asleep in his arms.

Eight

When Janine woke up, she stretched luxuriously. A sense of well-being made her skin tingle and her muscles tense and relax with remembered pleasure. Her hand searched for the warmth of Jacques's body next to her, but he was no longer there. The only sign of his presence was the slight depression his head had made on the other pillow, and the warm, musky odor of their lovemaking still lingering under the covers.

It had stopped raining and it was night. Through the open bedroom door, a faint light grayed the hallway, and from a distant room she heard reassuring sounds of dishes rattling. She slipped into the blue velour robe and padded barefoot toward the light and the sounds.

In the dining room, Jacques was lighting the sixth and last candle on the twin pewter candlesticks, then he moved a bowl of red and blue anemones to the center of the round, white damask-covered table. Unaware of her presence, he stepped back to admire the effect. The candles cast dancing lights on his blond hair and on the symmetrical planes of his face. Janine felt a surge of feelings engulf her. She loved this handsome man completely.

Smiling, she clapped her hands and said, "How beautiful everything looks."

He looked rueful. "I'm afraid that the table setting will be the only conventional item in our meal. You should've seen me picking flowers with a flashlight." He walked to her and clasped her to him in a close embrace.

"Once you said that conventional things aren't much fun," she teased, then she raised her face and nibbled his bottom lip. "Mm, delicious," she said.

He laughed and softly bit her earlobe and her neck, then moved down to her breasts, but in a second he pulled her robe back together and said, "This won't do at all. I'm famished." He led her to a chair and had her sit down.

"Let me help you in the kitchen. What would you like me to do?" she asked.

"For the time being, I only want you to eat what I'll put before you."

Grabbing the leg of his jeans and pulling him to her, she exhaled into his blue shirt. She laughed when she saw the goosebumps on his forearms and the blond hairs standing up as if electrified.

"Behave yourself," he said, walking away to the pantry.

After several trips, the table was laden with smoked oysters, caviar, crackers, hearts of palm, artichoke hearts, and pears in heavy syrup. A silver icebucket held a bottle of wine.

"This is a feast," she said.

"The feast was earlier this afternoon. Now we're just refueling. I'm sorry it's not a proper dinner, but we're several miles out of Ostend and I couldn't get anyone to deliver till later tonight. I didn't want to go shopping and leave you alone while you were sleeping."

After they finished their dinner, they lay on the cushions in each other's arms, drinking coffee before the blazing fire. Janine felt so contented that she was almost asleep again when the doorbell rang. She waited by the fire and listened to the voices coming from the back hallway where Jacques had gone to open the service door for a deliveryman.

In a few minutes Jacques returned with a blue paper sack. "Besides some groceries, I had these delivered. Come and see if you like them," he said, pulling out a pale yellow bikini and a dotted-swiss coverup of the same color.

She fingered the small triangles of material and said, "Very pretty. Thank you, Jacques. But I didn't know we were going swimming."

"I didn't either. As a matter of fact, I thought we'd return to the chateau tonight."

"And you've changed your mind?" she teased.

"You've changed my mind." He removed her robe and dropped it at her feet. His hands followed the curves of her body, cupping her breasts, then her hips. He clasped her to him and murmured in her hair, "About everything." Then he stepped back and said, "Come on, try on your bathing suit and see if it fits."

The yellow triangles barely covered her, and her bosoms swelled out of the skimpy cups. She slipped on the coverup, which reached just below her buttocks. He studied her with a quizzical expression, while the firelight at her back flamed through the dotted swiss, making it transparent.

"The length makes your legs look even more beautiful than they are, but I'm afraid I'd never let you go on a public beach in that bikini. I told the saleswoman to choose something that would appeal to a young American, but I think she went overboard. I don't want other men to ogle what belongs to me."

"Jacques, human beings don't belong to other human beings. That's slavery."

"No. That's marriage." He sunk into the softness of the couch and stretched his legs out before him.

"Not even then," she replied. Then his words penetrated her consciousness, and she swallowed. "What did you say?" Her voice was barely audible.

"Don't act so shocked. I said 'marriage.' You know, when a man and a woman promise to forsake all others, and he keeps her and bestows on her all his worldly goods, and she obeys him and all that sort of thing. That was a proposal, my dear."

Her ears hummed and her heart pounded in her chest.

He had said nothing about loving and cherishing. "Just a minute, Jacques. I never said I'd marry you, and as far as promising to obey anybody, that particular verb disappeared from the marriage ceremony years ago." She turned her back and, leaning against the mantelpiece, toyed with the Dresden figurine of a shepherdess. The pounding of her heart was so loud that she felt as if the earlier thunderstorm had returned.

"I'm not feeling very flattered," he said, coming up behind her and kissing her neck. "What's the matter? I thought that was what you wanted. I thought . . ."

"Look, Jacques, just because you were the first doesn't oblige you to propose to me." She pushed him away and went to crouch in a corner of the sofa, knees drawn up and hands clasped about her legs.

His laughter filled the room. "What a silly goose you are. Don't you want to marry me?"

His question had a striking simplicity, but she refused to answer it. She was convinced that he felt honor-bound to offer her marriage, and she didn't want to be his wife if he thought he was just doing his duty. Jacques was a gentleman, and perhaps he felt that at least he should make the offer, but he probably hoped she'd refuse. "You don't owe me marriage," she finally said.

"Who said anything about owing? If you don't want to be my wife, be honest enough to say so, but don't try to go off on some idiotic tangent and convince yourself I don't really want to marry you. If I didn't, I wouldn't have proposed." His voice was hard as steel and his eyes were cold and distant.

"It certainly seems very strange to me that you never thought of marriage till we made love."

"Does it occur to you there's hardly been time to come up with a proposal much sooner than now? Should I've asked you to be my wife when I met you at the pond, or perhaps the night you climbed into my window?"

"Jacques, don't be cruel. If I hadn't been a virgin, you

wouldn't have proposed. This is just a summer romance and its time is almost up. . . ."

He yanked her up and clasped her to him. Lifting her chin, his eyes bore into hers like icicles. "Don't you dare cheapen this by calling it a summer romance. Its time is not up and never will be. You're mine and you can kick and scream if you want, but I'll not let you go." He scooped her up in his arms and took her to the bedroom, while she kicked and pushed against his chest.

He dropped her on the bed, and she bounced up and down for a few seconds. With a sudden movement, he pulled at her coverup, which immediately came unsnapped. While she tried to fight him off, punching his chest and doubling up her knees, he yanked off the tiny bathing suit. Fear mingled with an unaccountable shiver of excitement when he lowered himself on top of her and pinned her arms above her head and inserted his knees between her legs.

"Let me go," she ordered, but the words were muffled by his fierce kisses.

"Forget it," he said, and his tongue began to play its magic on her neck and ears, sending shivers of desire down her spine.

Still she fought him, but the sensations she remembered so well from the earlier lovemaking were flooding back and making her feel weak and vulnerable. With his free hand he began to take off his clothes, and the zipper of his jeans scraped her leg. She stopped fighting and, with as cool and sarcastic a tone as she could muster, asked, "Are you in the habit of raping women?" Then she forced herself to lie limp in his grasp.

Sensing that she'd given up struggling, he threw his clothes off the bed and begun a tracery of kisses on her shoulders and breasts. Then slowly and lingeringly his tongue circled her navel, while his fingers began caressing her abdomen and her satiny inner thighs. "This is not rape," he growled. "I won't take you till you beg me to, Janine." Still kneeling between her legs, he grabbed a pillow and slid it under her hips. One of his fingers traced a slow, sensuous pattern at the upper end of her inner thighs.

At the sensations engulfing her, a sob escaped her clenched teeth, and she wanted to pull him down over her, but she was determined to resist his seductive touch and her own body, which was betraying her.

His hands moved to her throbbing center, and his tongue caressed, coaxed, and moistened her. She pulsated in the clutches of a fiery, consuming, raw desire, and her entire body begged to be possessed, but she only bit her lip and shuddered, unwilling to admit the power he had over her.

At his plunging, her moist membranes clutched his rhythmic touch, and still she tried to hide it, but he knew she had begun to climb toward the peak.

He turned on the bedside lamp, and she squeezed her eyes closed to shut out what was happening between them. But she couldn't hide her panting breath or the shivers of pleasure that made her body tremble.

"Look at me," he ordered, as he stopped all movement, all plunging, all trying to bring forth a release of tension from her. "Do you still imagine you don't belong to me and you don't want to be my wife?"

She looked at him through half-closed lids and moaned deep in her throat, while a shudder made her legs tremble. Squeezing her legs together, she closed her eyes again.

His voice compelled her once more. "Look at me. Look in my eyes and tell me you're not mine. Tell me you'll let some other man do this to you." Again his fingers began the rhythmic movements, and she couldn't sustain his gaze. She wanted to lose herself in the pleasure he was bringing forth from her body.

She arched her back, her hips on the pillow like an opened gift. She could only think of the burning desire that pierced her and throbbed through her. "Please, please, Jacques, don't torture me."

"But what sweet torture, *chérie!* Tell me now, as you look at me, that you don't want me." He lowered himself over her but didn't penetrate her. His hardness caressed and teased her vulnerability.

She wouldn't answer, but she grabbed his buttocks and pulled him inside her. As she let out a prolonged moan, she closed her eyes, trying to lose herself once more in the tidal wave that was lifting her up and up.

He didn't move inside her. Propped on his elbows, their bodies throbbed in stillness that was ready to erupt in a storm of passion. She squeezed the power that was claiming her as his own once again.

"Darling," he said huskily, "I want you to give yourself to me while you look in my eyes."

"Oh, Jacques, I can't!"

"Do it! I want to possess all of you, even your thoughts. I want to read the pleasure in your eyes as you surrender to me." He began moving very slowly at first, then the rhythm increased, while she held his gaze till she felt as if she belonged to him utterly and absolutely.

She finally closed her eyes as the sensations radiated from the center of her through each nerve path in her body. With a shudder of nearly unbearable pleasure, she finally relaxed under him, emptied and fulfilled.

Jacques lay over her, careful not to weigh too heavily, and when her breathing became less labored and her chest stopped heaving, he kissed her lips and said, "Lose yourself in me, sweetheart, just as I'm lost in you." Again he began his slow, rhythmic movements.

"Oh, Jacques," she moaned, her arms wrapped tightly across his broad shoulders.

"Am I hurting you?" he asked, stopping a moment and caressing her face. His gray eyes were like banked fires as he searched hers.

"No, but I feel as if I have no strength left in me," she said with a sigh.

"Just relax in my arms and let me make love to you," he murmured in her hair. Then he began kissing her gently and lingeringly, and she parted her lips and sucked his tongue into her mouth, as if she were prodding him on to take her completely once more.

His movements were like slow waves lapping the golden sands, then his motion increased like the sea at high tide. She wrapped her legs around his rippling muscles and was quickly engulfed in a raging torrent of sensations as she responded with such a concentration of pleasure that the lighted room disappeared from her consciousness and her body was the only reality in her world.

They lay exhausted in each other's arms through the night, and whenever she woke up for a second his warm, reassuring embrace was like a promise of future pleasure.

She woke up to see him standing by the bed wearing bathing trunks and a shoulder-buttoned, blue-striped sweater. He carried a tray and said, "All right, sleepyhead, here's your breakfast, then we're going sailing."

She sat up against the padded silk headboard and stretched. The sun streamed through the window and the sky was a brilliant blue over a barely ruffled, pearly gray sea. A sailboat bobbed at anchor in the shallow water near the beach.

"You ordered the day just for us," she said.

"Yes, just for us, *chérie.*" He smiled at her and set the tray across her knees. While she ate her bacon and eggs, he drank coffee, sitting on the bed.

Within a half-hour they were running free before the wind, the white sail balooning before them, while the graceful craft cut a fan-shaped wake, and the salt spray caressed their faces.

Janine followed Jacques's instructions and ducked to avoid the boom or leaned to one side with him to stabilize the boat till they were so far out that the villa was only a white speck surrounded by green. Then he furled the sail and dropped anchor. While the sailboat bobbed slightly in the gentle swell, and the heat of the sun filled Janine with warmth and contentment, Jacques took off his sweater and dived, cutting the water with such clean, perfect form that the sea barely rippled.

She joined him, and they swam away from the sailboat. At first the water felt chilly, but in minutes her skin was warm and tingly all over, and a feeling of well-being and power filled her every muscle. Jacques swam at her side, careful not to outdistance her, and within a half-hour they had returned to the boat and hung on to the gunwales to catch their breath.

"I feel so happy and whole," she said, running her hand over his shoulder. His skin felt smooth and cool, and his hair was softened and darkened by the water. Under her hands his muscles were like velvet-covered granite.

He kissed her lightly on the lips and said, "I like the salty taste, but then I like the way you taste all the time." He pulled the strap of her bikini off her shoulders and his mouth sought her nipples, sending a familiar thrill shooting through her.

Looping her arms about his neck, she gave herself up to the delicious sensation of his warmth against her cool flesh. The gently rocking sailboat was between them and the coast, and they bobbed in the water, clasped in each other's arms, with only the screeching gulls that wheeled overhead as witnesses.

"I've wanted to make love to you in the water since I heard your voice in the willow branches," he said, pulling off her bikini.

"Yes. That day at the pond, we were very close to making love. I wondered what it would be like." She fumbled with his bathing trunks, then dived underwater and slipped them off his legs. Trailing her mouth across his legs and abdomen, she popped out of the sea and found him laughing.

"It felt like a dolphin was nibbling at me," he said, and threw their swimsuits into the boat.

Under water, their bodies shimmered with a gray-green, evanescent light, and when he clasped her to him, she twined her legs around his hips without waiting for his prompting. He held on to the gunwale while she helped and guided him till they were joined, and he supported her hips with his other hand. The gentle swell of the sea rocked them in its embrace, and his mouth fastened on hers, while she moved faster and faster, starved for him, wanting him with all the pent-up passion of her days of waiting. She felt as if she were possessed by an unquenchable hunger for the marvelous, pleasure-giving body of this incredibly skilled, handsome man.

They reached the peak of sensation together, and she hid her face in the hollow of his neck and nuzzled him, murmuring his name, liking its sound, as if it were a hymn to the joy of their union. He held her close, and her only wish was that they could stay alone forever on the North Sea coast. She wanted the chateau, Kansas City, and the rest of the world to dissolve and never again intrude on their love.

The full moon cast a glow in the black sky and shimmered on the lake, reflecting the tawny walls of the chateau, when Jacques and Janine drove through the wrought-iron gates that night.

The butler met them in the entrance hall as they arrived. With a slight bow, he handed Jacques a telegram and said, "Monsieur and Madame Laurent are expecting you and mademoiselle for dinner, sir."

Jacques stuffed the telegram into his pocket without reading it. "Tell them we'll join them shortly," he replied, and hurried with Janine to the bedroom wing.

"Aren't you going to read it?" she asked.

"In a moment. We'd better hurry now. Wear the peach dinner dress, *chérie*. I can hardly wait for my father to meet you, and I want you to look your best when I tell them we're going to get married," he said, stopping before his bedroom door.

"Jacques, don't tell them. There's so much to talk about before we make that decision." She lay a hand on his arm and pleaded, "Besides, they'll know we've spent the past two days together, and I'll feel too embarrassed, especially on first meeting your father."

They'd both avoided the subject of marriage after he'd

first brought it up, and she'd felt as if she were living in a limbo of uncertainty. On one hand, she knew she'd never been as happy as when he made love to her, but on the other hand she still worried that all he felt for her was physical attraction and a sense of duty. Underlying these doubts was the nagging thought of leaving her own country and being the wife of a man who perhaps would soon tire of her and consider their union a mistake. She couldn't bear to think that he might ever be ashamed of her and regret his impulsiveness. She loved him, but was she ready for such a drastic and permanent change in her life? Why couldn't he move to Kansas City and give them a chance to know each other better? She remembered how brusquely he'd dismissed that suggestion before, and she hadn't dared bring it up again.

He saw that her eyes were filling with tears and caressed her cheek. "I think it would be best to have everything out in the open, Janine. Let me handle it my way."

"No, Jacques. If you say we're getting married, I'll deny it," she said, and rushed to her room to dress for dinner.

When side by side they entered an intimate salon furnished in Louis XIV style, Madame and Monsieur Laurent were sitting on damask-covered chairs on each side of a carved marble fireplace over which a Corot landscape echoed the colors of the upholstery.

Janine barely saw the attractive room. Her heart was pounding so loudly that she was afraid it could be heard by the others. More than anything she wanted to hold Jacques's hand for reassurance, but she stood straight, hands relaxed at her sides, her petite figure enhanced by the long-sleeved peach faille dress that fell in soft folds about her.

Nine

Monsieur André Laurent looked like an older version of his son—tall, erect, and aristocratic in his perfectly tailored dinner jacket. His blond hair had faded to silver, and his gray eyes were surrounded by a network of fine wrinkles, like the eyes of a sailor used to squinting across wide expanses of ocean.

He stood up and bowed slightly when he shook Janine's hand. "It's a pleasure to make your acquaintance, Mademoiselle Heerlen."

The butler announced that dinner was served, and Jacques escorted his stepmother, while Janine followed on the arm of Monsieur Laurent.

He patted Janine's hand and smiled. "You certainly have caused big waves for a ship of such small draft," he said as he looked down at her with a quizzical expression.

"Big waves?" she asked, and wondered what his wife had told him. He only winked in response, as if they shared a secret.

They sat at the long dining-room table covered by an ivory-lace tablecloth. The antique silver, crystal, and china sparkled in the light of the chandeliers, and a bowl of gardenias scented the room. The setting was formal and beautiful, but Janine had unpleasant memories of the dinner ritual. She hoped tonight's meal would go off smoothly.

While the butler served bouillabaisse from a steaming soup tureen, they chattered about horses, and Monsieur Laurent skillfully drew Janine into the conversation.

When the butler retreated to the pantry, and Janine was beginning to relax, Madame Laurent touched the cameo brooch at the neck of her black silk dress and said to Jacques, "The de Turennes send their regards." Then she turned to her husband and said, "Philippe wants to talk to you when he comes to the party next week."

"What about?" Andre asked, sipping his wine. His face showed a complete lack of interest.

"About Monette's dowry, of course," Francine Laurent replied.

Madame Laurent had dropped her bombshell. The spoon trembled in Janine's hand as she brought it to her mouth. Without raising her head from her plate, she glanced at Jacques and saw him scowling.

"Monette's dowry's of no concern, Father. I'll not marry her, and I'd appreciate it very much if you'd stop your matchmaking efforts, madame." Jacques's tone was irritated and cold.

"Jacques, you've agreed that it's time for you to marry. Monette's the perfect match. Just last month you didn't seem to object. It's just since . . ." Her voice trailed into silence and she looked to her husband for help.

"Francine, you know your niece wants to marry that young veterinarian. Why don't you and your sister stop making that child miserable?" Andre sounded annoyed. He turned to Janine with a courtly smile and said, "In your country, Monette and Monsieur Beaumont would have eloped by now. Isn't that so?"

Janine nodded, not trusting herself to speak.

"God forbid!" Francine exclaimed. "You know very well, André, that young Beaumont isn't a suitable match for her. Philippe and my sister have given their daughter the choice of either marrying Jacques or going back to boarding school. When I left this morning, she finally agreed to give up Francois. Now, Jacques, it's up to you. Philippe was so happy that he said he'd add a stand of timber in the Ardennes to her dowry." She looked from her stepson to her husband for approval. Monette's worth had increased with the added asset.

Hurt and embarrassed, Janine felt like leaving the dinner table and letting the Laurents talk privately. She swallowed a spoonful of soup without tasting it.

Just then the butler entered and began serving roast leg of lamb from a silver platter. The conversation shifted to Monsieur Laurent's purchase of a Renoir during his recent trip to London. But the new subject was dropped as soon as the butler withdrew.

"Madame, in order for a marriage to take place, both parties have to agree to the match. I don't want to marry Monette de Turenne and she doesn't want to marry me. I'm going to marry Janine." He looked from his stepmother to his father, and the expression on his face was hard and unyielding, as if he expected objections.

Madame and Monsieur Laurent stopped with their forks halfway to their mouths, and a heavy silence fell in the luxurious dining room. Through the open window the hooting of an owl seemed to underscore Jacques's statement, and Janine shivered at the bad omen. The hooting reverberated through the protracted silence.

Monsieur Laurent looked through the open french doors at the moonlit garden and said, "Well! Well!" while his wife started to say something, changed her mind, coughed, and stared at her plate.

It was evident to Janine that Madame Laurent was very upset and that Monsieur Laurent was at a loss for words. He cleared his throat and leaned back in his chair. "I've always been in favor of a love match, but have the two of you known each other long enough? Marriage isn't always plain sailing, and a sudden storm could swamp the most stable ship. You haven't set a date yet, have you?"

"We'll marry as soon as possible," Jacques replied; then,

turning to Janine, he asked, "Will two weeks give you enough time to get ready?"

Madame Laurent raised an eyebrow and, steepling her fingers, looked toward the beamed ceiling. "Is it a matter of . . . ? Is it because . . . ? Is Mademoiselle . . . ?" She couldn't find the words to ask her question.

Janine saw Monsieur Laurent studying her face and, feeling cornered, gave vent to her anger. She said, "Madame, if you're asking whether we *have to* marry so quickly, the answer is no!" Then she stared at Jacques across the table from her and, stressing each word for emphasis, said, "I've not agreed to marry you."

"You're more mature than your years, Mademoiselle," Madame Laurent said with a smile of relief. "Marital relationships are very difficult in the best of circumstances, and when a couple's backgrounds are as different as Jacques's and yours, you'd start out with several strikes against you. I think you're being very wise indeed."

The butler entered like a shadow and quietly served coffee and a chocolate torte covered with whipped cream. Madame Laurent started talking about her husband's collection of Impressionist paintings, but the prominent lines between her nose and her mouth seemed to have become more deeply etched during the last half-hour.

The atmosphere in the room was heavy, the conversation limped along, and Monsieur Laurent's attempts at humor fell flat. Janine's stomach ached and she felt nauseated. She avoided looking at Jacques.

They were almost through with their coffee when the butler told Jacques that a Monsieur Hennebique from Washington, D.C., was on the phone. Jacques went to take the call in the small salon next to the dining room, and just before the butler closed the door behind him, Janine heard him say, "Yes, Yves, I've received the telegram."

Taking advantage of the interruption, Madame Laurent pleaded a headache and excused herself. Janine thought that evidently the dinner conversation hadn't agreed with her either, but she'd chosen the controversial subject, and all four of them had suffered the consequences.

Just as Janine was about to follow suit and retreat to her room, Monsieur Laurent smiled at her and remarked, "Young lady, don't pay attention to what anybody tells you. Do whatever you think is right for you. You're the one who'll be most affected by the decision and you can't consider anybody's feelings but your own in this very important matter."

"Thank you, sir," she said.

"Don't misunderstand me now, Mademoiselle Heerlen. If you decide to marry my son, I'll be happy to have you for my daughter-in-law."

She was grateful to him for the kind words and the warm smile, but she still felt resentful toward Jacques for rising to his stepmother's bait, ignoring her own request, and subjecting her to the stress of the confrontation when nothing had really been decided between them. They should've ironed out their differences in private, then they could have presented a united front.

Excusing herself, she hurried to her room and locked her door. When an hour later Jacques knocked softly, she refused to answer. Leaning against the door, she listened to his steps retreating down the carpeted hall. When she heard his door slam, she sat on her bed and let the tears flow unchecked. They'd been so happy on the North Sea shore, away from all interferences. But now they were back in the real world, a world that focused on and magnified their differences.

In the morning, when the telephone on her nighttable rang and woke her up, it was already nine o'clock, and the sunlight shimmering on the lake designed wavy patterns across the bedroom walls. She hesitated to answer. She didn't want to talk to Jacques. Not yet.

When she finally picked up the receiver, Pierre Heerlen said, "There's a letter from the States at the house. Do you want me to forward it or do you want to pick it up?"

"I'll come and get it. Thanks, Uncle Pierre." The day

looked beautiful, and a walk would help her sort out her thoughts.

She arrived at the Heerlens' soon after ten, and was greeted by Heidi, who sniffed her legs and wagged her tail in welcome. No one else was in the house.

Janine was puzzled to see that the letter was from Mr. Hillman, the principal of Ellison High School. As she tore open the envelope, she smiled as she remembered how pleasant Mike Hillman had always been to her. He was an old friend of her father's, and she was sure their long-standing acquaintance had helped her obtain the teaching position. She sat down on the couch, her jean-clad legs tucked under her, and her smile froze on her lips. She flushed with anger as she read:

> Mr. Yves Hennebique, cultural attaché of the Belgian embassy in Washington, D.C., called me today to inquire about the procedures to be followed to release you from your teaching contract. I told him I'd have to have a written request from you. Please keep in mind that time is running short and I need to know immediately if I should replace you, or if you intend to honor your commitment. I hope you're well and nothing is amiss.

Janine threw the letter onto the coffee table, rushed to the telephone stand, and picked up the directory, but she was so upset that at first the listings blurred before her eyes. She finally found the number of Jacques's office in Nivelle and dialed. Unable to keep still, she paced the floor as far as the cord allowed.

When Jacques's secretary finally put him on the line, Janine was barely able to control her voice. "Jacques, I'm so angry with you, I don't even know what to say!" she spluttered.

"I know you're angry, *chérie*. You locked me out of your room and we wasted an entire night. I'd hoped that you'd have cooled off by now."

"You've cooled me off permanently, buddy! How dare you interfere with my job?" she shouted.

"I haven't interfered with your precious job," he shouted back. Through the receiver she heard a door slam, then his voice softened, and he said, "Please calm down and be sensible."

"I'm being as sensible as I know how. Everything's very clear to me. No wonder you wouldn't look at the telegram last night. You didn't want me to see it. You set out to deceive me."

"There was no point telling you about it till I was sure of my ground. I was going to tell you what I learned from Yves after I talked to him on the phone, but you wouldn't listen to me. You locked me out. Did you want me to break down your door?"

"Did it ever cross your mind to let me know beforehand what you were planning?"

"I told you there'd be no problem in getting you out of your contract, but you wouldn't believe me. I had to be sure so that we wouldn't get into another fight. Will you listen to me now?"

"No, I won't! It's quite clear to me that the fact that I've spent four years of my life to prepare for a career makes no difference to you whatsoever."

"But, Janine, how can we marry unless you stay here? Be reasonable."

"I suppose you think you're being reasonable, but I call it high-handed. I wouldn't dream of making decisions about your career. Why do you think you can do that for me?"

"Janine, is your job more important to you than I am? More important than the rest of our lives together?"

"What would the rest of my life with you be like if you can do such a thing? Now I'll start working under a black cloud. The principal really went to bat for me to get me that position." She ground her teeth in frustration. Jacques would never understand.

"You talk as if teaching high school were the opportunity of a lifetime. I thought I meant more to you than a paltry job!" He sounded as angry and frustrated as she was feeling.

"I don't even want to talk to you anymore and I don't know when and if I'll ever want to see you again. You take over everything! I haven't given you that right and I don't intend to—now or ever."

"Is that the way you really feel?" His voice was so cold that Janine shivered.

Was this the man who had made love to her? She remembered when they'd had their first real fight and made up in bed. Even the bed had become a battleground. He'd controlled her through her senses, and she'd forgotten everything but their lovemaking and the pleasure they were sharing. But there had been problems before, and his attempts to control her life had multiplied in spite of her objections. Now their unresolved conflicts were driving a permanent wedge between them.

"Yes," she answered, but her voice trembled.

"Are you telling me that you actually don't want to be my wife?"

"That's it! I'm unwilling to be your alter ego. I want to be my own person. From the way you've behaved ever since I met you, I can see the writing on the wall. My life would have to revolve around yours, and I don't want to live that way."

"You're making yourself perfectly clear."

"Great! Goodbye, Jacques Laurent!" She slammed down the receiver. Covering her mouth with her clenched fists, she stared at the telephone. Then the realization that she'd actually said goodbye to him filled her with a sense of irretrievable loss, and tears brimmed out of her eyes.

She threw herself on the couch and sobbed. When Heidi tried to nuzzle her hair, Janine pushed her away, and the dog lay by the sofa with her head between her paws and whined softly.

After a while, Janine walked to the window and through swollen, reddened eyes looked from the distant line of poplars to the old windmill. Everything reminded her of Jacques.

She shook her head and made her decision. The first teachers' meeting before school opened was only a week away. She might as well leave now. She didn't want to start her new job in an emotional turmoil, and she hoped that the familiar surroundings of home would soothe her and help her to put the recent events in their proper perspective. Jacques had a way of turning everything around when they were together so that any problem, no matter how serious, seemed to become insignificant. She had to get away from him.

After washing her face with cold water, Janine called the airline. She had an open-ended ticket and was told that she could catch a flight to New York at three o'clock that afternoon.

She telephoned the café. "Uncle Pierre, I need a favor," she said. Her voice was hoarse from the recent sobbing.

"Are you ill?" he asked, full of concern. Then he immediately added, "Sure, Janine. How can I help?"

She reassured him about her health and said, "I'm at your house and I want to return to the States today. Will you drive me to the chateau to pick up my things?"

"I knew there was something wrong this morning when Madame Laurent stopped at the café. She'd never come before."

Laure picked up the extension and said, "You should never have moved in with them. I told you, but you just wouldn't listen."

Yes, Janine thought, Laure had forwarned her, but that didn't help matters now. "What did Madame Laurent want?" She held her breath, afraid of the answer.

"We're not quite sure. She just sort of talked around things," Pierre answered.

"What things?" Janine knew from experience that Jacques's stepmother was an expert manipulator. Perhaps her refusal to marry Jacques the previous night hadn't reassured Madame Laurent.

"One thing she hinted at was that she'd prevail on her husband not to tear down our business, but that statement was sort of buried among a string of compliments about the charm of our place," he said.

"Pierre, didn't she say something about Janine leaving? I didn't connect the two things till after she left and I puzzled over her words. But really, the more I think about it, the more it seems as if our keeping the café depends on Janine going back home," Laure said indignantly.

Janine took a deep breath to calm herself. That woman was clever and ruthless. "We'll talk when I see you. Could you come after me now?"

"Is it urgent or can you wait a couple of hours, till I close up for lunch?" Pierre asked.

Laure interjected, "You go right now, Pierre. I'll look after the café. It'll be good to have you with us again, Janine."

Pierre hung up and Janine said, "I'm afraid I've already made reservations for my flight back. I have to check in by two o'clock."

Laure was silent a moment, then asked, "Won't I get to say goodbye to you?"

"Yes, Aunt Laure. We'll stop at the cafe on the way to the airport. I'm sorry."

"I am too. I knew no good would come out of your friendship with Jacques Laurent. I tried to warn you about how ruthless that family is, but never mind now. What's done is done. I'll see you in a little while." Janine heard a catch in Laure's voice, as if her aunt was trying to hold back her tears.

Janine left the keys to the Heerlens' house on the coffee table and walked to the lane to wait for her uncle. The metallic click of the gate closing behind her had a sound of finality. The doves cooed from the roof and from the chestnut tree, and the sunshine made the buttercups along the grassy verge shine with waxy brightness, but Janine could only think of the sun shining on Jacques's blond hair and on his bare chest as he sat his stallion with relaxed ease on that first day when he'd brought her back from the willow pond. She remembered that, as she'd listened to the sound of hoofbeats disappearing in the distance, she'd wondered if she'd imagined the encounter. Now she kicked at some gravel and bit her lip. He'd been real enough, and because of him she wasn't the same as when she'd first arrived in this Belgian village. She'd been a girl. Now she was a woman.

She heard a car, and a moment later her uncle's black Peugeot passed the old farmhouse at the fork in the road. When Pierre stopped before her and opened the car door, Janine forced herself to smile. There was no need to burden her relatives with her problems.

"I'm sorry to rush you like this," she said as they drove to the chateau.

"Don't worry, child. If it doesn't take you too long to pack, we'll have time to stop at the café so you can say goodbye to your aunt, and we'll still get to the airport in time."

At the airport, she was kissing Pierre goodbye and getting ready to place her handbag on the conveyor belt for its contents to be X rayed, when she heard the sound of running footsteps.

She turned to see Jacques elbowing his way through the crowd. His blond hair falling across his forehead gave him a disheveled look, and his unbuttoned suit jacket flapped with each step.

Pierre put his arm around his niece's shoulders and said, "You'd better go if you want to avoid a scene." He frowned as he looked at the line of passengers behind Janine.

"Janine, wait!" Jacques called, and with a final step was at her side. He grabbed her arm and pulled her out of the line. People turned to look and Pierre stared at the floor.

"Let go of me, Jacques!" Janine said between her teeth. She wished he hadn't come to the airport. In her heart she'd said goodbye to him when she'd placed a sealed farewell note on his pillow. She'd hoped he wouldn't find it till he went up to his room to dress for dinner, and by that time she'd be flying over the Atlantic Ocean.

"You can't leave till we talk things over." The scowl on his face and the piercing look in his gray eyes made Janine shudder in his grasp.

"I'm afraid your idea of talking things over is quite different from mine. You never listen to me. You only tell me what to do. I'm not willing to listen to you now." She tried to pull away from him, but he clutched her arm tightly. She looked at his hand and hissed, "See what I mean?"

He dropped his hand and murmured, "Why are you doing this to us?"

"I'm not doing anything to us. You're the one who has destroyed whatever I thought we had."

"But running away is no solution." He brushed the hair back from his forehead, and she saw a blood vessel pulsating in his temple.

Suppressing an impulse to touch his face, she said, "I'm not running away. I'm going back where I belong, where I have a home and a job. I'm following my original plans. Everything can't be your way. If I were foolish enough to listen to you, even the memories of what was good between us would be destroyed." She took a step toward the thinning line of passengers boarding the plane.

"I won't let you do this," Jacques said, taking her hand and pulling her back to him.

Pierre stepped forward and with repressed anger in his voice said, "Monsieur Laurent, please let go of my niece."

Janine yanked her hand out of his grasp and ran to the gate. The other passengers had been watching the scene and now stepped back to make room for her. She dropped her purse on the conveyor belt and walked through the barrier. She didn't dare turn around and wave at her uncle. She knew that if she looked at Jacques's gray eyes once more she'd never leave.

Ten

"I'll be there in a minute," Janine called from her kitchen, where she'd just plugged in the percolator. She tied the belt of her flowered robe and hurried to the front door.

The chimes rang for the third time as she raked her hands through her dark hair and wondered who was so impatient to see her at seven o'clock in the morning.

She opened the door and cried, "Monette! Francois! What a surprise! Come on in." She stepped back and the young couple walked into her house.

"We just got married," Monette announced, holding up her left hand to show off her wedding ring.

Janine kissed her and murmured, "I always admired your determination, but when your aunt took you back to your parents, I thought that was the end of your plans. The day before I left, she said you'd given Francois up." She led the way into the living room and opened the drapes. The early-morning sun shone through the leaves of a hanging fern and designed arabesques on the pale green carpet. That last dinner at the chateau seemed so far away. Was it possible that only two weeks had passed?

Monette plopped down on the gray suede couch and

tucked her coltish legs under her. Behind her hexagonal glasses, her blue eyes sparkled with green flecks of light, and her gray suit and coral blouse made her look like an ad of a honeymooning bride. "Where there's a will there's a way," she said, smiling at her husband. Her face glowed. She'd married the man she loved.

"I'm so happy for both of you," Janine said, and tried to swallow the lump in her throat. The smile she forced was little more than a grimace, and the dark circles under her violet eyes broadcast how poorly she'd been sleeping since her return. She missed Jacques so much that she'd begun to question her decision. The thought of him never gave her any peace, and she'd finally telephoned him two days before, but the butler hadn't seemed to know where he was. She'd left a message, but he hadn't returned her call. Perhaps it was just as well. What was there left to say? School started the following day, and she'd be teaching. Wasn't that what she wanted?

"You don't look happy. You look about as miserable as I felt the last time you saw me. And Jacques doesn't look any better. He loves you, you know."

Janine said, "He never said so." Then, feeling foolish, she stared down at her bare feet and murmured as if to herself, "But neither did I."

"Why did you leave so suddenly?" Monette asked.

"It's a long story," Janine replied, afraid that if she disclosed the details she'd lose control. "Let's not talk about me." She turned to Francois. "Congratulations. You were smarter than I was," she said, remembering the conversation they'd had at the lion monument in Waterloo. He'd not been too proud to change his mind and had married Monette in spite of all his doubts. Now he looked slightly sheepish, tired, and rumpled in his brown suit, but there was an unmistakable air of contentment about him.

He nodded. "Thank you," he said, moving closer to Monette and taking her hand in his. "We've Jacques to thank for helping us out." He looked down at the plush carpeting as if embarrassed.

Janine swallowed and breathed deeply to control the hammering of her heart. How foolish she'd been ever to think that Jacques might marry Monette. She adjusted the drapes to keep the sun from shining in Francois's eyes and sat down facing them. The aroma of coffee began spreading through the house.

Monette said, "I told Jacques I'm pregnant. My parents wanted me to have an abortion, but I refused." She squeezed her husband's hand when she saw him wince. "Come on, stop being so shy. Janine's our friend."

"Are you really expecting?" Janine asked. From the maple tree in the front yard a mocking bird sang of life, and joy, and love. Life could be so simple. Why was her own so complicated?

"Of course. I planned it that way. I couldn't let my lover's pride get in the way and keep us from getting married." She laughed and brought Francois's hand to her lips, then she proudly patted her flat abdomen. "Only six more months to go. But don't worry about us. Jacques fixed everything. He found Francois a job in a small animal hospital in Topeka and loaned us the money to get started. Actually, he gave us most of it as a wedding gift."

"What'll your parents do?"

"What can they do?" Monette shrugged. "I'm their only daughter. They'll come around, especially after they see their grandchild."

Janine looked at Francois. His face was flushed a deep red, but a hesitant smile turned up the corners of his thin lips. She said, "We both thought Monette would marry Jacques, didn't we? We were pretty dumb."

His smile widened when his wife said, "I was the only one who had no doubts. Once I know what I want, I go after it. The two of you, though, gave up too quickly. Not me . . . and not Jacques. I don't think you've seen the last of him, Janine."

Janine squeezed her hands together in an effort to control their trembling. "You don't know what happened," she said, remembering the scene at the airport. Jacques would never forgive her. She'd been as stubborn as a mule and now she was paying the price. Her independence was proving very costly.

"I don't have to know the details. I'm sure it was just a lovers' quarrel. Don't you agree, Francois?"

He raised his eyebrows and shrugged. "He didn't take me into his confidence. Sometimes things are much more complicated for men than they are for women."

Janine went to the kitchen to pour the coffee and thought about his statement. She'd been unreasonable to expect that Jacques could leave his family estate and follow her here. There was too much at stake for him. It hadn't been just stubbornness on his part.

When she returned to the living room with the steaming mugs of coffee, the young couple told her how they'd rented a car as soon as they'd landed in Tulsa. Following Jacques's advice, they'd driven straight to Miami, Oklahoma, where there was no waiting period to get married. A justice of the peace had performed the ceremony the night before, and now they were on their way to Topeka. Janine was the only friend they had in their adoptive country, but they didn't care. They had each other.

After they left, she dressed and decided to tackle a job she'd been postponing. Feeling like a hypocrite, she wrote to thank Madame Laurent for her hospitality. Buying a gift for her would be more difficult. The chateau teemed with exquisite objets d'art. What she wanted was something made in the United States that could hold its own and would need no apology.

She drove to the Plaza, and after two hours of shopping she finally settled on a blue Steuben dolphin. The graceful crystal mammal reminded her of the time she and Jacques had swum in the North Sea. When her lips had brushed his legs and abdomen, he'd compared the sensation to a dolphin nibbling at him.

While the saleswoman wrapped the gift for shipping, Janine wondered if he would see the dolphin and know what had prompted the choice.

When she returned home, she decided to mow the lawn to take her mind off Jacques. She missed him. She wanted him. At night she longed for his body next to hers. It would be a long time before she would stop needing him. Still, if she had let him take over her life, she would have resented him, and in the end her resentment would've destroyed their relationship.

She pushed the lawnmower diagonally across the yard, liking the geometric design it created. The smell of cut grass mingled with the scent of red roses that bloomed with a last burst of color against the split-rail fence. The roses reminded her of Jacques. Wiping perspiration from her forehead, she thought that she was as guilty of destroying the relationship as he was. She could've found another job, but she'd never find another Jacques Laurent. As she stored the mower in the garage, she noticed a blister on her palm. Self-sufficiency was taking its toll.

After another restless night and an exhausting first day of classes, as Janine unlocked the front door she heard the phone ringing. Throwing her keys and purse on the couch, she picked up the receiver. Her heart always skipped a beat whenever the telephone rang, but Jacques never called.

Tom Flowers, the editor of the *Johnson County Gazette*, boomed, "Janine, I just read your article about the Laurent vineyards and like it very much."

She slanted the receiver away from her ear. "Thanks, Tom," she said, remembering the effort it had cost her. With Jacques's notes and the photographs she'd taken of him, she'd felt as if his presence had invaded her home. Every time she looked at his picture on the chestnut stallion, it was as if she could still inhale the scent of wild mint and honeysuckle that grew in such profusion at the willow pond. But the notes and the photos were only paper, and the memory of his warm flesh haunted her empty bed at night.

"The pictures are excellent too, but we need some of the

winery in Lone Jack, Missouri. They'll enhance the local angle of the feature. Did you see the ad in today's *Star*?"

"What ad?" She plopped down on the armchair and kicked off her high heels. The newspapers had accumulated unread in the wicker basket at her side, and she'd been thinking of discontinuing delivery. She couldn't summon any interest in the news. The only news she wanted were news of Jacques.

"The one about the Laurent vineyards' grape-harvest festival this Saturday. It sounds like a big promotion. I'd like you to go. It's less than an hour's drive."

When she parked her white Buick Skylark in the sun-drenched graveled lot of the Laurent vineyards on Saturday afternoon, Janine was greeted by the sounds of bluegrass music and laughter.

She followed the crowd toward the old red-brick buildings on the far side of a hedgerow and snapped photographs of the grapevine-covered fields, the buildings, and a huge wooden vat set up in the middle of a close-cropped lawn. In the vat, several laughing young people bounced around and stomped on grapes, squirting the purple liquid over their clothes.

When he saw her taking pictures, and she told him the reason, a middle-aged, heavyset man, his khakis stained with grape juice, introduced himself to her as Bill Wright, the manager of the winery.

"I didn't know wine was still made this way," she said, puzzled by the scene before her.

"It's not. This is just a promotion. We're using the few concord grapes left in the vineyards and letting the kids have fun. This is the last of the concord-grape harvest. We'll be grafting new hybrid vines onto the existing roots so we won't have to replant. If you follow me, I'll show you the wine presses."

She followed him into the coolness of one of the buildings and took pictures of the wine presses. Their huge rollers reminded her of old-fashioned washing machines squatting in the shadows, and the scent of fermentation was like a thick, pervasive presence in the large rectangular room.

When Mr. Wright told her that the scent was from Leon Millot and Villard Blanc grapes, she felt goosebumps cover her arms. That day at the old mill, Jacques had told her that her skin and lips smelled and tasted like those grapes. She thanked the manager and hurried back outside, where she was again surrounded by music, laughter, and sunlight.

She watched a young couple wash their feet in a galvanized tub of warm soapy water, then step onto a plank leading to the wooden vat. They stood on the plank, laughing and jumping about while a red-haired young man in blue jeans hosed the suds off their feet and legs. When the couple stepped down a short ladder and joined the dozen people already in the vat, Janine wondered why she felt as if she'd witnessed the scene before. She smiled when she remembered an old "I Love Lucy" show she'd seen long ago.

The bluegrass band began playing "Oh, Them Golden Slippers," and the people in the vat stomped in time to the lively tune, while the redheaded youth called to the laughing crowd, "Step right up, folks, and get a free bottle of grape juice."

Bill Wright filled bottles with foamy purple liquid from a spigot on the side of the vat. Corks, glass tubes, and short lengths of tan rubber hose displayed on a long folding table were for sale together with a booklet on winemaking.

Janine was having a good time as she clapped her hands, tapped her feet to the catchy, familiar tune, and watched four couples on the lawn before the bandstand improvising a square dance that one of the men called in a high, piping voice.

"Come join the fun, miss," the redheaded fellow said to Janine as he pointed to the merrymakers in the vat.

"Why not?" she said, and handed Mr. Wright her camera. She stepped out of her sandals, and pulled the back of her skirt between her legs and tucked it in at the waistband in front so that it looked like a pair of pantaloons.

Another girl joined her on the bouncing board, and they giggled and shivered at the shock of cold water on their soapy legs.

As soon as she stepped into the vat, the band started playing a tune about an old mule, and the mandolin player sang and invited everybody to join in the refrain of "Hoheeho, heeho, heeho."

Janine stomped, laughed, and joined the rest of the crowd. Her feet and legs turned purple, and a glob of mashed grapes splattered on her white blouse. Just as she threw her head back to join the chorus once again, her voice died in her throat, and her heart did a somersault.

Perfectly groomed and dressed in gray flannels and a navy blazer with gold buttons, Jacques approached the vat and watched her.

"What're you doing?" he asked with thinly veiled horror.

The grapes squished between her toes, and her feet slid about in the pulpy mess. A picture of the marble and gilt rooms of the chateau, of elegant dinner clothes, of servants silently scurrying about, and of conversations about operas and plays flashed through her mind and contrasted so sharply with these down-home surroundings that for a second she froze as if suspended in a dream. Which life was real? She filled her eyes with the look of him—so handsome, so correct, so aristocratic, and so incongruous in this setting.

The people about her jostled her, and the noise made her ears buzz, while her toes curled in the grape pulp.

Bill Wright whispered something to Jacques, who nodded, but his face showed complete amazement. When Jacques replied, his manager smiled at Janine and walked away toward the bandstand.

Over the hubbub, Janine called to Jacques, "It's your promotion! You tell me! I'm just having fun. I might even take home a bottle of grape juice and make some wine. I haven't had a wine cooler in a long time."

"If that's what you fancy, then that's what you should have," Jacques said evenly.

Janine stuck her chin up in the air, and once again joined the other singers and brayed defiantly, "Hoohheeho, heeho, heeho!"

What was happening to her? She'd so much wanted to see him, and now that he stood before her, she was needling him. Was she really caught up in the harvest festival, or was she punishing him for the inadequacies she'd felt within herself at being unable to adapt to his culture?

Now it was his turn to experience culture shock. This was his vineyard, but she was in her own country, and these were her own people. She laughed when she saw him cover his eyes. Lone Jack, Missouri, was as foreign to him as Orpe Le Petit, Belgium, had been to her.

When he looked up, he said, "I've heard about the stubbornness of mules, but I never connected it with you before. You're right in your own element."

Janine slipped and grabbed the rim of the vat. "I'm no more mulish than you are. Are you just going to stand there? Is it beneath your dignity to join the peasants?" she taunted.

Jacques quirked an eyebrow, and for a second a crooked grin softened his face. He'd picked up her challenge and was going to show her his willingness to accept her culture. When Bill Wright returned, Jacques removed his blazer and handed it to him.

As soon as the banjo player saw Jacques take off his tie, he spread his arms wide and said over the loudspeaker, "Look't what we got here, folks—a male stripper!"

Girls squealed, giggled, and clapped, while the banjo player started humming, "Dum, dum, dum, dada, dum," and the bass picked up the beat of the "The Stripper."

Janine's eyes grew wide as she watched Jacques remove his shirt. His face was serious, and his lips didn't even show the beginning of a smile, but his gray eyes were laughing when he handed Bill Wright his shirt.

He bent down to remove his Gucci shoes and tucked his socks inside them. His burnished gold hair fell across his forehead when he rolled his gray slacks up above his knees, and Janine felt her heart fill to the bursting point with loving him.

"I'd have chosen a different meeting place," he said as he walked across the wobbly plank. He didn't wince as the stream of cold water hosed down his feet and splattered dark blotches on his gray slacks.

"Yes." She smiled and stretched her arms toward him.

He took her hand and twirled her about, and when she faced him again, he clasped her to him. She felt his body tremble against hers. Her arms looped about his neck, and he bent down and found her lips. Suddenly the laughter about them ceased, then the silence was broken by enthusiastic applause.

Janine and Jacques pulled apart and grinned at each other, while the crowd smiled, and the band started playing, "My luve's like a red, red rose."

"I've felt like the last rose of summer since I left you," she whispered.

"I know, *chérie*. Let's go home now, shall we?"

"Home?" she asked.

"To your house. Wherever we can be together is home," he said as he helped her out of the vat.

As soon as he closed the front door behind them, she walked into his arms. "How long are you going to stay?" she asked, afraid of the answer. On the drive back she'd kept watching his silver Corvette in her rear-view mirror, afraid he'd been a vision she'd conjured.

"As long as you let me." His lips caressed her forehead, her cheeks, her eyes, and his hands cradled her hips close to him.

"I'm so sorry, Jacques, about everything. I tried to call you to tell you how much I missed you, and when you didn't return my call, I thought you were through with me."

His kiss stopped her rush of words, and his tongue searched the inner recesses of her mouth with tender probings. A familiar thrill coursed from the roots of her hair to the tips of her toes. Forgetting all about the future, she gave herself to the exquisite sensations that flooded through her. Her fingertips fumbled with the buttons of his shirt and one popped off.

He laughed. "You don't have to tear off my clothes, *chérie*. I'm willing and eager." He nibbled her ear.

With passionate intensity she flamed at his touch. "Come on, Jacques," she said, and pulled him toward the bedroom, shedding her blouse and skirt as she walked across the living room.

The bedroom was bathed in the reddish flow of sunset when they lay side by side on the pale blue sheets. Their clothes were strewn like a path across the carpeting.

Propped on an elbow, she looked down at him, hardly believing he was really here. Her hand raked through the blond hair on his chest and caressed his taut muscles. "I thought I might never see you again."

He took her hard nipple in his mouth and eased her over him. With his muscular, warm length beneath her, she felt as if every nerve in her body were humming with a separate pleasure of its own. "Didn't you know I'd never let that happen?" he said huskily.

She shook her head. No, she hadn't known. The fear came rushing back, and she slipped her hands under his shoulders and clasped him to her trembling body.

"Don't be afraid. We'll always be together," he said as he gently pulled her legs apart. His gray eyes smoldered with unrestrained desire, and she grasped his back and buried her face in his neck, inhaling the warm scent of him.

Joined together, they moved with abandon to the remembered, ecstatic melody of their lovemaking as they took and gave of each other. All differences, arguments, and plans were forgotten in the heightened sensations of this moment they'd both craved since they'd last made love in the rocking swell of the North Sea.

Afterward, they lay in a close embrace while the setting sun looked like a flaming sphere outside the bedroom window. Copper glints brushed the tree trunks, and an unreal, flaming light bathed the room. even the shadows were smoldering coals. A rose-scented breeze cooled their damp bodies, and their skin seemed to have absorbed the incandescence of the sun.

He stroked her heaving breasts and kissed her brow. "I've thought about the things you said. I did try to control you, and when you balked I almost treated you as an adversary."

"I felt powerless and ran. We should've reached some sort of compromise."

"It seems we both forgot that our common goal was to be together. I'm used to having my own way, but I've come to realize that our life can't be just on my terms. I don't want to deprive you of the chance to prove yourself. I won't have a dissatisfied wife on my hands."

"Dissatisfied?"

"*Chérie*, when things go wrong in a marriage, sex seems to wither and die. We don't want that, do we?"

"No, we don't want that," she echoed. She nibbled his shoulder, liking its salty taste. With a finger she traced a path around his nipples, laughing when she saw goose-bumps rising on his skin.

"Can we get married tomorrow?" he asked, staring at the ceiling. He breathed very softly as he waited for her.

"Tomorrow?" Her violet eyes opened wide.

"Will you answer my question, Janine? I love you and I'll never let you go. That's not negotiable."

She snuggled closer to him. He'd finally told her he loved her, and even though she was happy to hear the words, they'd really not been necessary. Deep in her heart she'd known the truth. "And I love you, darling," she murmured as she caressed the firm line of his jaw. "Yes. The answer to your question is yes, yes, yes!"

"That's a relief. I was afraid."

"Afraid? You? I didn't think you feared anything."

He kissed her temple and said, "Don't make fun. I'm human, you know. The past weeks've been sheer hell."

"That's behind us now."

"At long last," he said, and cleared his throat as if to hide the vulnerability she'd glimpsed. His tone became businesslike. "All right, then. Tomorrow we'll drive to Miami, just like Monette and Francois did. Then I'll move in with you."

"But, Jacques, you can't leave Belgium. You have too much at stake. I can't ask that of you."

"Neither one of us'll have to make a great sacrifice. Why do you think you didn't hear from me these past weeks? It takes a while to make all the arrangements. My father has agreed to look after the estate for the next few months, and I've hired an assistant for Monsieur Charcot, our agent. I'll fly back a couple of times, if I'm needed. If you want, you can go with me during Christmas vacation. Then, in September, we'll move back to Orpe Le Petit, if you agree. Perhaps by that time you'll have had enough of teaching, and I can prevail upon you to be a lady of leisure." He rubbed his thumb across her palm and, feeling the blister, looked at her hand and frowned. "How did this happen?" He sounded as worried as if the small sore were a serious wound.

She chuckled. "Mowing the lawn. I suppose that'd be forbidden to a lady of leisure."

"Sheep keep our lawns cropped, but you can do all the gardening you want."

Thinking about the chateau, she was silent as she remembered Madame Laurent. Could they ever live under the same roof? Eat at the same table? The very thought of that made her feel queasy.

Misinterpreting her silence, Jacques said, "I told you that you can teach in Brussels, if that's what you really want to do, but somehow I feel you'll be too busy supervising the servants and enjoying our children." Propping himself up on an elbow, he gazed down at her and brushed the damp tendrils of dark hair from her forehead. "Unless, of course, you don't want children."

"But I do . . . our children. The children of Monsieur and Madame Jacques Laurent," she said dreamily. Then she remembered Les Alouettes and grinned. "Isn't it strange to think that my descendants'll own the land of my ancestors?"

"I thought about it. The deed to Les Alouette'll be my wedding present to you."

"What about this house?" She was very attached to it. It was the only home she'd ever known.

"Keep it. We'll live here from June till after the grape-harvest festival in September. The children'll learn to love this country, just like their mother does. How does that sound to you?"

He was painting a rosy picture, and she felt uncomfortable bringing up an unpleasant subject. "I'm concerned about your stepmother. She really doesn't like me, Jacques."

"Don't worry about her. She and my father live in Brussels and only stay at the chateau one month during the summer. We won't be there then. We'll be here. Besides, she's a realist. She'll be pleasant enough once you're my wife. And my father—he really likes you, you know. He refers to you as 'Our American Beauty Rose.' "

Janine laughed and stretched her arms above her head. The room was nearly dark, and the leaves of the birch trees etched against the purple sky quivered with golden highlights.

Jacques nibbled her ear and growled, "What about dinner? I'm famished. Let's go to a restaurant."

She sat up and swung her legs off the bed. "You might as well get used to an American Saturday-night dinner at home, my love. I'll get some steaks out of the freezer and fix a salad. Will you light the barbecue?"

Grinning sheepishly, he answered, "Of course, but you'll have to show me how the first time." He pulled her back down.

She ran her hand down his body and felt his desire for her reawakening. "It'll be midnight before we eat," she teased, and pulled him over her.

"It doesn't matter at all," he said.

When his mouth closed over hers, and his hands grasped and guided her hips, her last conscious thought was that he'd been right. Her home was in his arms.